SUMMERSIDE LAKE

MASSACRE

A slasher horror

L. R. J. ALLEN

L. R. J. Allen is an avid fan of the fantastic and has been addicted to popular fiction from a young age. He worked eight years in local government and four in telecoms before turning his hand to writing.

He lives outside Salisbury with his fiancée, Charlotte, and their cat Bella.

First Edition

This is a work of fiction. Names, characters, places, and incidents either are the products of the author's imagination or are used fictitiously. Any resemblance to actual persons, living or dead, businesses, companies, events, or locales is entirely coincidental.

Cover design created by Placeit and Book Brush

Typeset 10 Plantin, 16 Another Danger
ISBN: **9781650298610**
Imprint: **Independently published**

This one is dedicated to the trinity of influential slasher filmmakers:

John Carpenter
Wes Craven
Sean S. Cunningham

And for Charlotte.
Always.

AUTHOR'S NOTE

This is not elevated horror.

There is no pretence here that this is anything other than a throwback to the heyday of the slasher boom of the early 1980s, so if you're expecting some kind of commentary on the genre or a black comic edge like *Scream* then you will be disappointed.

What this is, however, is an unironic 80s set homage that aims for the jugular. There is violence, sex, nudity, and a lot of blood that is either instigated by or directed against camp counselors.

This is not high art nor is it intended to be. If you go into a book titled *Summerside Lake Massacre* expecting otherwise, then you've come to the wrong rodeo.

To everyone else, enjoy.

SUMMERSIDE LAKE

MASSACRE

PROLOGUE

1959

The sun was making its final pass behind the fir trees that surrounded Summerside Lake, casting beautiful fragmented golden rays over a carpet of lush grass that made up the shore of the small cove. The cove in question was neither large nor intrusive despite being entirely artificial.

It was constructed at the behest of Wallace Asher, a relatively young and spirited local entrepreneur with ambitions of fame during the summer of 1958, his aspirations spurred by his family's wealth. Upon completion the cove was noted for its tasteful adherence to the surrounding landscape while the location allowed for entirely unobstructed view of Summerside Hills, the nearest town, which was home to some ten thousand residents.

The cove was the centrepiece of Camp Summerside, a recreational space that could accommodate up to one hundred and fifty guests. The camp contained three large huts built for fifty guests each, a medical hut that also housed the administrative offices and CB radio, and an imposing main hall that was used for gatherings and dining.

So it was, in the summer of 1959, nearly a full year after construction began, Wallace Asher stood proud among the press as he posed for photographs with construction workers and the eight counselors that would be working at the camp for the summer. He smiled as he stood at the entrance, itself an arch made of the same mahogany as the surrounding buildings, a cigar lodged between his teeth, and brandishing a set of oversized scissors. It was noted in the press that the venue's grand opening was a relatively slight affair, as Asher himself was usually a man of few words, but the obvious pride in his creation was infectious.

"Welcome everybody!" he boomed to the waiting crowd. "Thank you all for attending. It's been a long, sometimes arduous, and often expensive process to get to where we are today but get there we did! As such, I will keep things brief. To those I need to thank, I will thank you all in person. But, for now, I declare Camp Summerside officially open for business!"

Asher beamed as he cut the gaudy red ribbon among polite applause and clicking camera shutters.

There were none there that day that could say an ill word of the event. It marked a new chapter in the history of Summerside Hills. The tranquil lake would gift the youth of the neighboring areas a place of frivolity for the hot summer months.

SUMMERSIDE LAKE MASSACRE

The year of 1959 would be a year that no one in Summerside Lake would forget. Unfortunately, however, it would be for very different and altogether more gruesome reasons.

1984

The view was one of controlled chaos as Deputy Elias Ansel of the Summerside Hills Sheriff's department arrived on scene. Save for a string of festoon lights circling the central green that dominated the view from the main entrance, the only lighting was the persistent flashing of red and blue.

The entrance arch itself would have been grand on any other occasion. Made entirely of mahogany, the arch was weather worn and the once vibrant colors of its signage were in desperate need of a new coat of paint, yet there was no mistaking the inimitable bold letters embossed in the two-metre oval logo that sat at the top of the arch:

CAMP SUMMERSIDE

Est 1959

SUMMERSIDE LAKE MASSACRE

It was through this archway that death loitered.

Deputy Ansel pulled up behind one of the ambulances and exited his cruiser. The vehicles were parked next to each other and two young counselors sat in the back of one being tended to by numerous paramedics.

As he walked to the central green, he was struck by just how grim the spectacle was.

There were multiple small teams of forensics tackling the scenes of murder. At the centre of the green was a large pool of coagulated blood, on which rested a severed foot. It still wore its shoe. One of the forensic team squatted and gingerly lifted the dismembered appendage before placing it into a clear evidence bag.

To Elias's right, just outside the large main hall, were seven body bags placed side by side in a neat line. The man he wanted to see was squatted beside the one furthest to the left.

"Sheriff," Deputy Ansel called.

The Sheriff looked up and beckoned him over.

"What the hell happened?" Elias asked.

The Sheriff pointed down to the open body bag at his feet. A familiar, although dead, face peered blankly from it.

"Him?" asked Elias incredulously.

The Sheriff nodded. "This is all his doing. Poor kids barely stood a chance."

Deputy Ansel felt his gut tighten as he looked along the line of body bags.

"That's not all," the Sheriff said. "Wallace Asher is also

dead."

"Asher? The guy who owns the camp?"

The Sheriff nodded.

"We found his head in the main hall. No sign of his body yet but we're searching."

The Deputy stared at the appalling scene around them.

Twice in one night? He thought. *What is happening to this town?*

PART ONE

THE COUNSELORS

"Death has come to your little town, Sheriff."

Halloween, 1978

ONE

Three days before the massacre, Sheriff Doug Clark sat at his desk in the Summerside Hills police station awaiting a phone call from the County Prosecutor.

The hour was late, and the Sheriff's department was quiet, which was how Doug liked it.

Now approaching his mid-fifties, Douglas Clark had been a resident of Summerside Hills his entire life, his family having fled to the pacific northwest from the antebellum south during the civil war. Back then Summerside Hills was little more than a hamlet of small wooden shacks centred around the church that doubled as a village hall.

It was the lake, though, that was the deciding factor for Clark's descendants. It was unlike anything they had in the south and with the neighboring forests and the endless hills, it was the perfect place to settle down and start anew.

That was not to say it was easy. Although the north boasted

of their abolition of slavery with pride, that did not mean prejudice had disappeared. Their choice of settlement had mostly white faces: the Clark's were still seen as black first and people second.

They had prospered though. Despite challenges, the Clark lumber yard was founded and was still a significant company within town. The yard's success bought with it prestige and influence and by the time Doug had his first interview to become a county Deputy, the Clark name had arguably become as integral to the town's history as the lake on which it resided, a feat the incumbent Sheriff had come to resent. Much to his annoyance, his bid to become Sheriff had been somewhat easy and while his relative youth and previous job as the acting managing director of the family's company had undeniably benefitted from his name, his want to be Sheriff was born not out of ambition but from a strong moral backbone. He wanted to help the town that had supported his family, to give back to the community in the grandest way possible, and what grander a way was there than to head the town's Sheriff department?

The moment that sowed the seed for the younger Doug Clark to one day become Sheriff had been in his late twenties.

The county's summer camp had opened across the lake when a gentleman named Karl Molyneux, a well-liked individual and hard worker who was kind to his neighbors and attended church every Sunday, slit his wife's throat with a bread knife before walking into town and killing a further eight people. It was the darkest chapter in the town's history and still raw to many.

SUMMERSIDE LAKE MASSACRE

Doug enlisted in the Sherriff's department the next day and within a week had been deputised. He worked thirteen years as a deputy, amassing a tremendous service record and an affable relationship with the residence he felt privileged to serve. It was not always easy; his time as a Deputy resulted in neither a wife or a family, though he had wanted both, and his lack of influence allowed for little in the way of reforms he felt the department needed.

Which was why, when the opportunity arose, submitting his candidacy for Sheriff seemed like the most obvious progression for his career.

He did so in 1972 when the previous Sheriff, a cantankerous old man named Clancy Wydell, known for his often belligerent nature, retired. Doug himself was forty-one at the time and many saw him as a bright and youthful shift from Wydell's iron fists.

And, of course, his name held weight. He could not deny that his success was owed in large part to his surname. Respect, however, was still an earned commodity.

There were many that doubted his abilities to act as Sheriff. Managing a logging company was far removed from the responsibilities of law enforcement and the mere fact of being a Clark did not entitle him to becoming the face of the county's Sheriff department.

To Doug's credit, he tackled these criticisms head on. In an impassioned speech outside of the Summerside Hills town hall, he spoke in earnest of how his family had arrived all those years ago looking for refuge without a penny yet had built their way up to where they were today.

"Summerside Hills has been good to the Clark family," he had said, "and I want to continue giving back."

While he still had his sceptics, the speech did the trick. He ran unopposed at the beginning of 1973 to become the county's new Sheriff.

He would be lying if the enormity of his new responsibilities had not been daunting. There was much he had to prove to his doubters, something he would have relished demonstrating had he had an opponent to run against. But the job was his, and for that he was certainly grateful. And while the stress had, at times, added more grey hairs and defined his wrinkles, it was a responsibility he was willing to shoulder for the good of the community.

However, the good of the community, at present, required him to be sat behind his desk, awaiting an important phone call.

The County Prosecutor, Clive Barstow, was a person Doug tolerated at best and plain disliked at worst. Though he was loathed to admit it, Clive was a ruthless attorney and a valuable man to keep on side.

If anything, Doug's dislike stemmed from a clash of perspective. While he would not class the man as immoral, there was an honour that Barstow severely lacked. County Prosecutor Clive Barstow was a man that cared more about self-image and promotion than the rule of law, and while he had never attempted anything illegal - to Doug's knowledge at least - the

Sheriff would not be surprised to hear if illegality was involved in the pursuit of a win.

Doug sipped his stale coffee, his seventh of the day, with his feet on his desk when the phone finally rang. He peered at the clock hung above the entrance to his office. It was 5:45pm.

He lifted the receiver.

"Sheriff Clark."

"You can skip the formalities Dougie," came the whiney voice on the other end of the line, "I won't be long."

"Call me Dougie again and I'll have you arrested," said the Sheriff, resentfully.

"Yeah, yeah," said Barstow, bored, "look, I've just got off the phone with Judge Atwell and he can't see any further reasons for delays. They want him moved by the end of the week."

Doug gripped the receiver tighter and exhaled. It was the result he was expecting but not the one he was hoping for.

"The defence…" he began.

"The defence outplayed us, pure and simple. I could argue until I'm blue in the face but the Judge ain't budging, ok? Of course, we can appeal but you know as well as I how long that's gonna take."

"And a postponement?" asked Doug hopefully.

"It probably won't come in time to stop them moving him." Doug could hear the frustration in Barstow's tone. He was unaccustomed to defeat.

"Look, I'm sorry Doug," Clive continued, "I really am. But this one is gonna have to play out while we lodge an appeal, and we won't get that done before they move him. Come Friday, they want him transferred upstate."

Upstate, Doug thought, *to that cushy all-inclusive hotel they call minimum security. What kind of punishment is that?*

"Doug, you there?" asked Barstow.

"I'm here," said Doug. He took another sip of his coffee and continued, "listen Clive, go home, ok? Come to my office first thing tomorrow and we can discuss our options."

"You really don't want to let this slide, do you?"

"No, I don't. But neither does the town. The people here don't forget so easily."

Clive chuckled and said, "Never a truer word spoken. I'll speak to you tomorrow Chief."

Doug opened his mouth to respond but the line was dead.

He leaned back in his chair and folded his hands behind his head. Clive would arrive in the morning fresh faced and ready to fight but, of course, the prosecutor was quite correct. Even *if* they filed a postponement on the ruling, the likelihood of it appearing before a different Judge in time to stop the transfer was zero. The law moved slow in these parts, and no amount of good will Doug had earned could make it move any quicker.

He stared at the clock above his door and sighed.

"Shit," he said.

TWO

Although the induction pack stated the venue as the Town Hall, the reality was far less exciting and somewhat demoralizing.

When Gillian approached the Hall's main entrance, she was greeted with a hurriedly written note on crumpled paper that was stuck to door at face height. It read:

ALL SUMMER CAMP BUSINESS!
PLEASE HEAD TO THE ANNEX TO THE RIGHT OF
THE MAIN ENTRANCE!

There was another sheet of paper stuck next to the first with a crudely drawn arrow pointing to Gillian's right, though she was unsure as to whether she needed to enter the building and then turn right, or to turn right from where she stood. She opted for the latter.

The town hall was not a large building yet over the years additional extensions had been added to expand its functionality. The front façade retained the old-town aesthetic that was still prevalent around much of Summerside Hills, yet many of the additional spaces were modern and gaudy - at odds with the original building.

As Gillian rounded the far-right corner of the hall's exterior she was met with one these gaudy extensions, although calling it an extension was giving the structure too much credit. It was made up of what appeared to be two temporary office cabins bolted together, which was attached to the main hall. The structure appeared flimsy at best and far less robust than anything found in a trailer park, as if a stiff breeze would break it. In fact, as Gillian continued to stare, she saw they *were* trailer park trailers, just hollowed out and painted grey.

There was a makeshift wheelchair ramp that led to an entrance that, had it been used as someone's home, would have been the patio doors. Stuck on the wall next to the entrance was another hurriedly written sign with a basic rendering of the Camp Summerside logo, hand drawn of course, and big, bold lettering in black permanent marker that said:

COUNSELOR INDUCTION HERE!

Gillian's shoulders sagged as she pulled her backpack tighter and strolled toward the open patio door.

"Hey!" came a voice from behind her, "is this the right place for camp induction?"

Gillian turned to see a confused young man stood a few feet from her, clutching what she recognised as the same invitation she had folded neatly in her back pocket.

He appeared nervous, unsure of himself, as if his existence would be a nuisance to anyone he was in immediate proximity of. It was a trait she could spot instantly: it was one she also shared, though she had developed a thick skin built on quick wit and sass. The man was also quite short, shorter than Gillian at least, herself only five foot six. He wore a white and sky-blue striped t-shirt that seemed impossibly bright against his ebony skin, beige cargo shorts that stopped at his knees, and yellow sneakers with white socks pulled halfway up his shins. The crowning glory, however, were the thick rimmed glasses that sat awkwardly upon his face.

He'll be eaten alive, Gillian thought.

She smiled.

"I guess," she said, "although I was expecting it to be in the main hall." She fished the folded invitation from her back pocket. "Says so on here."

The kid smiled back and said, "I know. Confusing, isn't it?"

He held out his hand.

"I'm Nick," he said earnestly.

Gillian took his hand in hers.

"Gillian," she replied, shaking Nick's hand.

"A whole summer at Camp Summerside huh?" Nick said. "I can think of worse ways to get paid."

"Wait, you're getting paid?" asked Gillian, her face dropping.
Nick went pale.

"What?" he asked with a tremor in his voice.

Gillian laughed.

"I'm just fucking with you Nick," she said, smiling. She was met with an uneasy laugh in return.

"Seriously though," she continued, "it should be fun. I'll admit, I've never done this before. I'm kind of new to the area."

"You're not from Summerside Hills?" asked Nick, apparently shocked at this revelation.

Gillian shook her head and said, "Seattle, born and bred, though the city was getting too much for my parents. Honestly, it's been crazy getting used to just how quiet it is around here."

Nick smiled.

"I like the quiet," he said, "although I'm sure the sounds of nature will get tiring very quickly once we're on the other side of the lake."

"It's that close?" asked Gillian.

Nick frowned.

"You really aren't from around here, are you?" he said.

Gillian shook her head and said, "Can't say I've had the grand tour."

Nick nodded and turned from her to face the street outside the hall.

The hall itself was situated roughly two thirds up the hill on which the town resided. It afforded a terrific view of the lake and surrounding woodland and as the sun beamed down from the cloudless, mid-morning sky, the reflections on the water were serene and beautiful.

Nick beckoned Gillian over and pointed out toward the lake.

"See that?" he asked.

Gillian leaned forward and squinted.

"What am I looking at?"

"The far side of the lake, about halfway along the shore?" said Nick. "You should see a small cove and a bunch of huts."

Gillian tracked his finger until she saw what she was looking for. It was small but noticeable, a patch of vibrant green with the occasional dot of mahogany that Gillian assumed were the accommodation structures. Now she saw it, she was surprised she had never noticed it before. It stood out like a siren against the darker hues of the forest around it.

"That's Camp Summerside?" she asked.

"That's Camp Summerside," Nick said. "About two miles from here as the crow flies. If we're lucky they'll ferry us out across the water, otherwise it's a fairly uneventful car ride around the lake. Not quite as fun."

"You know, I've not been on the lake yet," said Gillian.

"Oh, you should! You can hire a paddle boat or a kayak for as long as you want. People spend hours out there swimming or fishing or just chilling in the sun."

Gillian looked at her new acquaintance with a curious smirk while Nick stared out at the water with joy. It was quite sweet really, Gillian thought, to meet someone that appeared so happy over something so small.

Nick noticed her staring and flushed.

"What? What did I do?" he asked nervously.

"You're ok Nick, you know that?" said Gillian.

"I...am?"

"You are," Gillian said, smiling.

Nick smiled awkwardly back, stared down at his feet, and clumsily fixed his glasses. Gillian guessed his interactions with girls his age were relatively few.

"You know..." Nick started.

"You two here for the induction?"

Both Gillian and Nick turned to see a preppy man at the annex entrance. He stood with his hands on his hips in a wide legged stance. The crease in his brow emitted an air of seriousness that sucked the energy from the moment Gillian and Nick had just shared.

"Christ Chad don't be such a sourpuss, man!" someone called from inside the annex as another man appeared to Chad's right. This man, compared to Chad, was smiling and wore a tailored, pinstriped suit. He appeared older too, with Gillian guessing the man was in his mid-twenties.

"Ah! Our final two!" the man said, slapping his companion on the shoulder. "Well, c'mon, come meet the others!"

He quickly turned on his heels and waved them into the annex. Chad, his face stern, simply grunted and followed.

Gillian turned to Nick who shrugged. She shrugged in return, a giggle escaping her, and the two of them walked toward the annex and their induction as camp counselors.

THREE

The conversation Sheriff Clark had with Clive Barstow's opposite number went about as well as expected. The chief defence attorney was one of three and Doug could never remember who was who. The call came in not long after Barstow's and was filled with several platitudes and commiserations behind a thinly veiled smugness that Clark detested. The Sheriff offered his congratulations while also making his own thinly veiled barbs.

The following morning, around the time that Gillian was waking to prepare for her counselling induction, Doug was in his office and already on his second cup of coffee. He was pacing, a sign to his deputies and secretary that he was not to be disturbed, while he awaited the arrival of Barstow.

As he sipped his coffee and considered topping up his cup, he noticed his secretary, Janet, approach his office with a familiar man in what was fast becoming a worn and battered suit.

Janet knocked twice before opening the door.

"Clive Barstow, here to see you."

"Thank you, Janet."

Janet nodded and stepped aside, letting Barstow pass her into the office, where he threw himself into the chair across the desk from Doug's. Janet looked to Doug who merely shook his head. His secretary nodded with pursed lips and walked briskly from the office.

As Janet closed the door, Doug asked, "Coffee?"

Clive waved a hand dismissively.

"You know I don't drink that shit," he said.

"I figured you'd have been up much of the night after our call," said the Sheriff.

Clive sighed and shook his head.

"Suit yourself," said Doug as he grabbed the coffee pot and poured himself another. He did not hurry back to his desk and as he stirred his drink needlessly, adding neither sugar nor milk, he could see the prosecutor growing increasingly agitated.

Doug took another tentative sip, walked to his side of the desk, and sat down.

"Have anything for me?" he asked.

The man opposite him appeared troubled and sleep deprived. His suit was creased as if he had slept in it, which was likely, and his face was pale. Barstow's hair was the only thing he had seen to that morning, it seemed. It was neatly combed, slicked back, and unmistakably reeked of pomade.

"I filed a postponement before I came in," Clive said. "I

wouldn't get your hopes up though."

"I won't, but I appreciate it."

"Don't expect any last-minute miracles either," Clive sighed.

"You always told me you were the miracle maker."

"I'm fresh out of those and, frankly, fresh out of fucks to give."

The Sheriff had never seen the prosecutor so despondent.

"So, that's it?" Doug asked.

"That's it," Clive pulled a red pack of Marlboros from the inside pocket of his suit and put one between his lips before offering one to the Sheriff. Doug waved the offer away while sliding an ash tray across the desk. Clive lit his cigarette and exhaled deeply. The gentle blue smoke rose in soft wisps, dancing upwards until it mixed with the dust motes floating in the morning sun. The silence between the two was only broken by the sounds of birds singing and the muffled tapping of Janet's typewriter.

"You know," Clive began, "I'm not too used to losing. It's happened once or twice but I don't think it's arrogant of me to say that I'm generally good at what I do."

"Agreed."

"But while I was on my way here," the prosecutor continued, "I got to thinking. Is what's happening the most terrible thing in the world?"

Doug frowned.

"What do you mean?" he asked.

Clive tapped his cigarette over the ashtray and a clump of ash silently fell.

"Your boy, he'll still be locked away you know?" Clive said.

"Locked away?" said the Sheriff. "Have you seen the facilities at that place? It's not just minimum security, it's a Hilton."

"That may be, but there're still bars and armed guards-"

"And tennis courts and a recreational swimming pool and oil painting classes. They're sending him to an early retirement home."

"He's kept his nose clean all this time," said Clive.

"That doesn't negate what he did," Doug retorted.

Clive shrugged and exhaled smoke from his nose.

"May I ask you something Sheriff?" he asked. "Just between us boys."

Doug leaned back in his chair.

"By all means."

Clive nodded, leaned forward, and stubbed out his cigarette before pulling another from his packet and lighting it.

"Neither of us were in our respective games when Molyneux did what he did. You were working for your old man and I was fucking my way through college."

"Your point being?"

"My point being that neither of us had anything invested in this."

"Speak for yourself," said Clark.

"C'mon Doug, don't give me that," said Barstow. "You have Wydell to thank for putting Molyneux where he is today and it's not like you owe that miserable old fool anything."

"Not Wydell, no. I don't owe him anything. But it's my duty to this town as the Sheriff to ensure that Molyneux stays where he is."

"And you don't think his new digs will work?"

"I don't think his new digs are appropriate for the crime."

Clive nodded.

"I agree, but it grieves me to say that Judge Atwell disagrees with both of us." Clive leant back in his chair and his whole body went slack. While Doug would never show it he felt every bit as deflated as Barstow appeared.

Clive stubbed the second cigarette out and stood.

"I guess you'll need to make arrangements for Friday?" he asked.

Doug nodded and said, "We have a transport bus that I intend to have Molyneux handcuffed to the back seat of."

"How many deputies?"

"Two, plus the driver."

"Surely only one will do? The guy's hardly Michael Myers."

"It's the transfer of a very dangerous prisoner Clive," Doug said sternly, "I'd fill the bus with armed guards if I could spare the manpower."

The prosecutor held up his hands defensively.

"I wasn't criticising," he said. He stretched and stared at his watch.

"And what will you do with the rest of your day?" asked the Sheriff.

"Smoke my way through the rest of my smokes and have a

37 | P a g e

few bourbons I think."

Doug looked at the clock above the door.

"It's not even 10am," he said.

"Perks of being your own boss Dougie boy," Clive said with a smile.

Doug opened his mouth to speak.

"I know, I know," said Clive, "you'll have me arrested."

He turned and walked to the door.

"Enjoy your drink," Doug said, somewhat bitterly.

"I'm drowning my sorrows chief, but I'll do my best." And with that the lawyer was gone.

FOUR

The annex was not quite as miserable as Gillian had feared and there was an amiable atmosphere that suited her just fine.

She was surprised by the space. The floor was faux wood panelling and the walls had a deliberately aged quality that gave a rustic and cosy feel. The only furniture of note was a circle of ten chairs, half of them occupied by people she did not know, and two fold-out tables with an assortment of snacks, the kind you would find at a child's birthday party.

The man in the pinstriped suit was stood next to a much older gentleman who the others seemed well acquainted with. He appeared a man out of time, or so his dress sense told Gillian, though he and the younger man were easy friends it seemed. They were standing close to one another and engaged in a jovial but quiet conversation.

She leaned in toward Nick.

"Stay close to me," she said, "I don't know anyone."

"Really?" said Nick.

"How do you know them?" she asked.

"Sorry," said Nick, tapping himself on the forehead to emphasise his stupidity. "Forgot you're new. We all know each other from high school. We just graduated senior year at Summerside High. Apart from Chad, he's a few years older. I hear he has his eyes on being manager of the camp someday."

"He does?"

Nick nodded.

"He was a jerk at school, to be honest," said Nick. "I avoided him, but he was pure alpha dick-wad through and through. Kinda guy that will say high school was the best time of his life."

Gillian looked at Chad and tilted her head inquisitively.

"He looks harmless to me," she said. "Maybe a bit serious but I bet he's a pussycat really."

Nick grumbled something under his breath that Gillian ignored.

The older man looked over at Gillian and Nick as they loitered in the doorway.

"Come on in!" he beamed enthusiastically and waved them over. "Please, take a seat, we'll get started in a moment."

Nick smiled and offered Gillian his elbow.

"M 'lady?" he asked.

Gillian smiled back and linked her arm in his.

"Good sir," she said.

The two strolled confidently to the rest of the group, who

were all talking except for Chad, who was sat apart from the group. There were four others, strangers to her, and she hoped there would be formal introductions soon enough.

There were two seats together and as they took their places, Nick to Gillian's left, the girl to her right leaned in and offered her hand.

"Hey!" she gushed. "I'm Lucy. How you doing?"

Gillian was immediately disarmed by her delightful and earnest smile. There did not appear to be any artifice to her pleasantness and her smile radiated her natural beauty. She was also at total odds with Gillian. Where Gillian's hair was ginger and wild, Lucy's was a dark brunette and perfectly styled. Where Gillian's eyes were a soft mix of green and brown, Lucy's were stunningly blue, both piercing and quizzical.

Gillian, conscious of her gawping, took Lucy's hand and shook it.

"Gillian," she said, smiling.

"Oh my god, can you believe summer's starting already?" Lucy replied as she looked over at Nick. "Hey Nick," she said.

Nick waved awkwardly back and blushed.

Lucy returned her attention to Gillian.

"So, you must be Rebecca's replacement," she said.

"Rebecca?" Gillian asked.

"Guessing you don't know her then?" said Lucy, still smiling.

"I just moved here from Seattle," said Gillian.

"Oh cool! I always wanted to go to Seattle! That must be why I don't' recognise you." Lucy tousled her hair and continued.

"Rebecca was supposed to be helping out this year, but she ran off with Mitch, her boyfriend. Kind of a spur-of-the-moment type thing. I'm glad you were able to join us though. It's always great seeing a new face in town!"

Lucy placed a friendly hand on Gillian's shoulder and leaned back slightly toward the guy sat to her right. "Brandon," Lucy said as she gently nudged the man with her elbow. "Hey, Brandon, come say hi."

Brandon turned, placing the brochure he had been reading on his lap, and smiled. Gillian became immediately certain that he and Lucy were a couple as Brandon placed an affectionate hand on Lucy's thigh, giving it a gentle squeeze.

He was handsome in the same way as Lucy was beautiful. His mousy brown hair was loaded with product and slicked back, much like Chad's. And his smile was just as disarming as Lucy's

He looked from Gillian to Nick.

"Hey Nick! Who's the red-head?" he said with a wink.

"I'm Gillian," she laughed, blushing slightly.

"I'm guessing you're Rebecca's replacement?"

Gillian nodded. "Apparently so," she said.

Brandon opened his mouth to say something further when there was a short, loud clap before the group. All heads turned to see both the older man and his younger counterpart in the pinstriped suit smiling at them.

"Welcome," said the older man, as he strolled to one of the two remaining seats. The younger man took the seat next to Nick.

SUMMERSIDE LAKE MASSACRE

"Welcome and hello to you all," the older man continued. "Allow me to introduce myself. For those of you that don't know, I'm Wallace Asher, I'm the owner of Camp Summerside and, for this summer at least, your boss."

There was a murmur of laughter among the group.

"But don't let that put you off. Honestly, I'm a push-over really," more laughter, "but that's not to say we don't take things seriously around here. So, allow me to get the boring necessities out of the way.

"This summer marks the twenty-fifth anniversary of the opening of Camp Summerside, and it's been a great success. But, for it to have been a success, we have done so by amassing an exemplary safety record. So, while this summer will be filled with fun, let's be honest; who *doesn't* want to get paid for playing games all summer? We intend to maintain that safety record this year, and the next, and until the day that Camp Summerside closes."

There were nods of approval among the group.

"But you'll be happy to hear the rigours of safety training won't begin until we head to the camp tomorrow. Today is simply an introductory session for us all to get to know one another.

"I'm also aware that a number of you already know each other. That was, in part, the reason you were chosen this year. However, for the benefit of myself and my colleague here," he nodded to the younger man in the suit, "when I point at you, please give us your name and tell us a little bit about yourself.

"And we'll start with," he pointed immediately to Chad, "you!"

"I'm Chad Edwards," the boy said "You all probably remember me from school. This is my third year working at the camp and hopefully not my last."

"Excellent!" beamed Wallace. "Say hi to your dad at the *Gazette* next time you see him!"

He pointed to the girl at Chad's left. "And you dear?"

To Gillian the girl looked as though she did not want to be there and struck her as the kind of person whose personality was defined by her dress sense. In this instance the woman looked as though she could not decide whether she was Madonna or Cyndi Lauper. She stared at Wallace as if he was a bug that needed killing and obnoxiously chewed her gum.

"I'm Trixie," she said, non-committedly. Wallace's smile faltered as Trixie allowed the silence to become uncomfortably long, the only noise the overly loud smacking of her lips as she chewed her gum.

"Why don't you tell us a little about yourself?" Wallace asked.

Trixie folded her arms and shrugged.

"I'm just here to get paid," she said. There was another moment of uncomfortable silence before Wallace gave up and pointed to the man sat on Trixie's left.

"How about you?"

The man, much like Trixie, had a rebellious dress sense. His sleeveless denim jacket showed off his muscular arms, and his torn black jeans were barely held together. Gillian thought his attitude was childish and a little pathetic. To judge by the look on Wallace's face he had come to the same conclusion.

"I'm Marco, and Trixie's mine," he said. As he placed a hand on Trixie's thigh, Gillian was sure she saw her pause slightly before placing her hand on top of Marco's.

This seemed to be all the information Marco was willing to part with.

Wallace cleared his throat and continued across the group.

"And yourself?"

"Hi, I'm Brandon," he said happily. "Like most of you here, I'm Summerside Hills born and bred, and after the summer I hope to do some travelling."

"Very admirable," said Wallace already pointing to Lucy.

"I'm Lucy, and I'm gonna make sure Brandon stays out of trouble while we're travelling." The comment drew a snort of derision from Trixie that Lucy heard yet chose to ignore. She linked her arm with Brandon's.

"We haven't decided on where or *when* to go on our travels but somewhere in Europe sounds good," she said.

Brandon leaned in toward his girlfriend and whispered, "I thought we'd decided on Australia already?"

Lucy smiled and continued, "Well, maybe, Europe. We'll see where the mood takes us.

Brandon did not hide his frown. If Lucy noticed, she did not let on.

"Well, I hope you both have a great time wherever it is you go," Wallace said earnestly through the awkwardness.

He pointed to Gillian.

She waved at them all sheepishly.

"Erm, well, I'm Gillian. I'm new to Summerside Hills. I only moved here in April and my parents said I needed a summer job, so here I am."

"Ah! You must be Rebecca's replacement," Wallace said.

"Yes, so everyone keeps telling me."

"Well, we definitely appreciate you coming in. And what a great way to get to know the others!"

Gillian could not help but smile. Wallace's enthusiasm was infectious, if exhausting.

"And finally," he said pointing to Nick.

"And I'm Nick. You all know me from school-"

"Small dick McNick," sniggered Marco. Gillian stared at him in disgust, though whether he noticed or cared she could not tell. She could see a smirk on Chad's face.

"Wow, that wasn't old the fiftieth time you said it, No-Grow-Marco."

Marco's smile disappeared in an instant.

"Say that again nerd," said Marco as he clenched his fist until his knuckles went white.

The younger man, who had remained quiet during the introductions, rose to his feet.

"Now, now," he said calmly. "Let's not get at each other's throats on the first day, shall we?" He stared at Marco with a smile that conveyed more authority than warmth.

"Whatever," said Marco, but Gillian could not help but

notice him look away all the same. Trixie was visibly tense beside him.

"Right, well," sputtered Wallace. "I'd say that's the perfect time to introduce this rather well-dressed man before you. As the saying goes, I'm not getting any younger. While these last twenty-five years have been fruitful, it is high time that I spend my twilight years in retirement. As such, I have passed the baton. So, without any further ado, I'd like to welcome Mr Conrad Ellis, the new owner of Camp Summerside, to the team. Let's give him a hand!"

Wallace began clapping in earnest while the others produced a smattering of applause that was forced rather than agreeable. Conrad stood. If he was awkward at all with the introduction, he hid it well.

"Thank you, Wallace," he said. "And hello to you all. I'm Conrad and, as Wallace has said, I will be taking over the running of Camp Summerside from this year.

"So, you might be wondering what is likely to change? I would like to say right now that the only thing changing in terms of how we run things is that the face of your boss will be much younger than before."

There were some giggles from the team, honest ones. Conrad, it seemed, had a knack with people.

"Wallace will be around of course," he continued, "and should there be anything I'm unable to help with, he will be at hand to help under an advisory capacity."

Conrad turned to Wallace and said, "I also hope that you'll

be a regular face around the camp over the coming years. It is your baby after all."

Wallace nodded with a smile.

Trixie raised her hand.

"Yes?" Conrad asked.

"You're not from here." It was a statement.

Conrad smiled.

"You are quite right. I'm not a Summerside native. Much like Gillian here I moved to town not long ago. I'm from upstate New York, not far from Yonkers."

"Then what the hell are you doing here?" said Trixie argumentatively.

"Now, now," piped in Wallace, "that's no way to speak to your new boss."

"It's alright Wallace," said Conrad, "it's an honest question." Gillian noticed that grin again, the one he had shown Marco.

"I'm here for a major change of pace, honestly," he said. "I'm a city boy by birth and have lived around New York city my whole life. I can also say, without ego, that I've done quite well for myself. But if you live that fast twenty-four seven it eventually catches up with you and I found I didn't want to live like that anymore. So, I moved to your pleasant little town. I do get itchy fingers though, and I'm always in search of a new project to dive into. I heard that Wallace here was looking to retire so I figured why not?"

"So, we're a project now?" said Marco.

"Such cynicism with you two!" Conrad said in mock outrage,

though Gillian was unsure how artificial it was. "It's camp! You are literally getting paid to have fun for the summer! Isn't that something to be happy about?"

Marco shrugged.

"Well, you're definitely a project of mine now," said Conrad to Marco. "My goal is to get you to smile before the summer is over. How does that sound?"

Marco raised an eyebrow.

"That sounds like a bet," he said.

Conrad smiled.

"You know," he said, "it does, doesn't it? What's your surname young man?"

"Why?"

"We need to make it all official."

"Official?"

"Have you never made a bet before?"

"Not 'officially', no."

"Well, to do so we need each other's full names."

Marco shrugged.

"Lopez," he said.

Conrad walked to Marco, stood before him, and held out his hand.

"I, Conrad Ellis, bet that I can make you, Marco Lopez, smile before the end of the summer season."

Marco looked at the outstretched hand.

"And if you lose?"

"I jump fully dressed into the lake," Conrad said.

Marco gave him a suspicious look before taking his hand in his.

"It's a bet," he said.

"Excellent." Conrad turned to the rest of the group and said, "And now the introductions are out of the way, how about some food?"

FIVE

Clive Barstow was nursing a double Buffalo Trace on the rocks when the lead lawyer for the defence team, Bob Turner, entered the bar. Barstow was met by the sudden stench of Old Spice before a hand slapped him on the shoulder.

"Clive, my boy! Old habits die hard I see?"

The defence's main lawyer was a man not much younger than Clive and no less arrogant in his abilities. The two had known each other since law school and, for Clive, Turner had been a bad stench he could not seem to shake. Throughout his career their paths would cross until, eventually, Barstow learned that Turner had settled in the neighboring town. The town itself, MacLaughlin Springs, was a bitter rival to Summerside Hills in many ways, such as their high schools, football teams, and cheerleading squad, as well as jurisdictions when it came to the law. To find that his nemesis had moved to the one town that all

Summersiders despised did not surprise Clive and he would not have put it past Turner to have made the move deliberately.

Bob Turner was a short yet rotund individual. At only five foot seven his stature would have been considered slight were it not for the two hundred pounds of intrusive fat he carried. His chin blended effortlessly into his neck as a bulbous protrusion that was made more distinct by the tightness of his shirt collar. Where Clive appeared scruffy due to lack of sleep, helped in no small measure by the imbibing of whiskey at such an early hour, Turner cultivated a deliberately unkempt aesthetic that was emphasised by his scraggly and often unwashed hair and permanent stubble.

Clive took a sip of his drink and stared ahead.

"Commiseration always calls for the hard stuff," Clive said.

Turner sat his enormous frame on the stool next to Barstow, waddling into a comfortable position like an anthropomorphic walrus. He beckoned over the barman.

"Same as my friend here please and a bowl of peanuts," he said. The barman nodded.

"Come to gloat?" Clive asked.

"Naturally, but I also wouldn't miss the opportunity for midday drink."

The barman placed a full bowl of peanuts in front of the lawyers. When Clive did not reach for them, Bob shrugged and took the bowl for himself.

"You know the postponement will fail, right?" he asked Clive.

SUMMERSIDE LAKE MASSACRE

"It was never meant to work, it was just meant to stall," Clive answered.

"Your Sheriff has a real hard on for his guy, doesn't he?"

"A guy that killed his wife and eight other people for kicks? I'd be pretty set on keeping in the mad house too." He continued sipping his bourbon as Turner's drink arrived.

"Look, I get it ok?" said Bob as he chewed his peanuts. "And in fairness, the chances of him ever being released are small. But if we can at least make an exemplary inmate's twilight years a little bit better, I'm all for it."

"How admirable. I didn't realise you did this out of the kindness of your heart."

"I did it for the publicity Clive. I couldn't give a fuck who Molyneux is or what he did."

"You've managed to rile an entire town that see him as the boogeyman."

Turner shrugged.

"I'm not about to discuss the ethics of this with you," said Bob. "Besides, so long as you're a resident of the Hills and I'm in the Springs, you can guarantee I'll be watching your cases with renewed interest."

Clive downed the rest of his drink and ordered another.

"So, it's not just the publicity then," he said. "It's pettiness and spite too."

"No, not spite. It's never spite," Bob said as placed the last of the peanuts in his mouth. "Pettiness, sure, but spite?" He shook his head, took his drink, and downed it in two quick gulps.

Bob gingerly wobbled off his bar stool, reached into his right pocket, and pulled out a twenty-dollar bill that he slapped onto the bar.

"A word to the wise," he said to Clive. "Word around town is that your man Doug will receive a call from Atwell."

Clive frowned and turned to his rival.

"About what?" he asked.

"The postponement will be thrown out before mid-afternoon today and the Judge wants things to move fast. He's going to strongly advise the Sheriff to make the transfer tonight."

Clive's eyes widened.

"Tonight? I'm not even sure that's possible!"

"Hey, I'm just the messenger," Turner said.

"But it's not that simple. There'll need to be a couple of deputies allocated to the transfer at a minimum, the asylum will need to be notified and their security ready, the new prison will also need to be notified and made ready for the inmate, not to mention that there's a mountain of paperwork that will need to be completed before any of this can be started. Want me to continue?"

Bob nodded yet appeared bored.

"That is all true but, frankly, Atwell doesn't care. He doesn't see it as the usual judicial sense and feels it's dragged on long enough. The Sheriff can scream the house down, but I can all but guarantee that, by tonight, Molyneux *will* be on his way to Spring Hill Correctional."

Turner placed a quarter on the bar and slid it toward Clive.

"Give your man a call," he said before placing his hands in his pockets and whistling as he strolled merrily from the bar.

Clive stared bitterly at the quarter before beckoning the barman over.

"Hank, I need to use your phone," he said.

★

In the Sheriff's office, Douglas Clark's door was firmly shut as he continued his heated conversation with the Judge.

The call from Barstow had been a shock and, rather than wait for the supposed discussion with Judge Atwell, the Sheriff had called him immediately.

Yes, the judge wanted the transfer to be done that evening. Yes, he was aware of what it entailed. No, he could not be swayed from his decision. The Judge had, frankly, lost all patience with the continued longevity of the case. Karl Molyneux would be moved to the Spring Hill Correctional facility from Lake Side hospital for the Criminally Insane that evening, and if he was not in Spring Hill before midnight the Sheriff would appear in court the following morning to present just cause for the reasons of any further delays.

The Sheriff gripped the phone until his palms were sweaty. There were a number of legal avenues he could now pursue against Atwell, many of which he would put into motion once the call was over. However, like all matters within the legal system, these would take time and time was not a luxury that

Doug currently had.

He would do what the Judge said. He would do his duty to ensure that Molyneux was transferred with the utmost urgency. That did not mean, however, that Clark had any intention of making the Judge's life easy for the foreseeable future.

"Do we have an understanding?" asked Judge Atwell.

"We do your Honor," Doug said through clenched teeth. "I do, however, respectfully disagree with every aspect of this request."

"And I respectfully don't give a shit," the Judge said tersely. "I want this business with Molyneux done with. Clear?"

"I'll make some calls," said Doug.

"Be sure you do," said the Judge before slamming the phone against its cradle.

The Sheriff stared at the silent telephone before pressing the receiver with his finger and dialling extension 01. He could hear the phone ringing on the other side of his door as his secretary picked up.

"Sheriff," she said.

"Janet, could you see me in my office please?"

She was at his door two seconds later.

"Yes?" she asked.

"Who do we have off duty today?"

"I'm not sure but I haven't seen either Foster or Pratchett this morning. Ansel may be available too."

Clark nodded and stared at the clock above his door. It had just gone midday.

"Call them and say I need them in by 2pm. Tell them it's serious."

Janet frowned.

"There's seven other deputies working today," she said.

"And I'd rather not take them off their duties or let them know what we're doing. Once word gets out the town won't be happy."

"And what are we doing, if you don't mind my asking?" She straightened her glasses nervously.

Doug sighed.

"Karl Molyneux got himself a new residence."

SIX

The food was basic; pre-made sandwiches, Cheetos, and Twinkies, as well as all manner of other unhealthy and artificially preserved sustenance. Yet the food was free and other than a couple of sarcastic remarks from Trixie and Marco, the group remained amiable as they plated up their lunches.

The counselors split into their respective couples. Lucy and Brandon sat back in the circle and giggled with each other as young lovers do. Trixie and Marco went outside and disappeared behind the annex. Chad gravitated toward Conrad and Wallace.

Gillian and Nick made their way to the main atrium of the town hall where they found a bench and sat. Despite the time of day, it was surprisingly quiet, with only the receptionist, a kindly old lady who wore half-moon spectacles and looked brittle, for company. The silence around them coupled with the cavernous nature of the hall amplified even the smallest of sounds to a persistent echo.

Gillian stared around the space aimlessly. Apart from the bench on which she was sitting and the large ornate reception desk there was little in the way of anything that could be considered interesting. There were numerous plaques dedicated to members of the community whose names Gillian did not recognise nor did she particularly care of their exploits. The walls were bone white with a series of dark mahogany beams along the ceiling, which gave the hall a stark and somewhat soulless ambience.

"So, Marco's an asshole," she said after swallowing a handful of Cheetos. Despite the softness of her voice, the echo still felt as though it ricocheted off the walls.

Nick, who was also staring into space, nodded in agreement.

"Yes, he is," he said. "He's always had an attitude but since he got with Trixie it's gotten much worse."

"Ah, couple's feeding off one another, that kind of thing?"

"I guess," said Nick.

Gillian looked at him and saw him tensing.

"You and Marco have history," she observed.

"We used to be friends. Well, kind of. When we were in kindergarten. We were the only kids in our grade that weren't white, so we stuck together."

"What happened?" asked Gillian.

"He became an asshole, that's what happened." He took a bite of a stale tuna sandwich and continued. "Kids will look for anything they can latch onto to make another kid miserable. He didn't want being the only Mexican kid in class to make him a target, so he quickly bit back before anyone could bark."

"Leaving you in the dust?"

"Pretty much," said Nick. "Fortunately, being black was only a minor reason for being targeted. Turns out my glasses and my love of comic books were also a factor."

"Because you're a nerd?" asked Gillian.

Nick frowned, hurt, and turned to chastise his new companion before seeing the earnestness in her eyes.

"Don't call me that," he said quietly.

"Why not?" she asked.

"It's not nice."

Gillian raised an eyebrow.

"Why isn't it nice?" she said.

"Because it's nasty and I don't like it ok!" Nick snapped before blushing and staring at his shoes. The receptionist looked up from what she was reading and shushed them. Gillian waved her an apology before leaning in close to her new friend.

"Who makes being a nerd a bad thing? Marco?"

He nodded and said, "Among others."

"And how about anyone that *isn't* a bully?"

"No, actually," he said, sounding surprised. "Come to think of it I don't hear it from anyone else."

Gillian smiled.

"Being a nerd isn't a bad thing," she said, placing an arm around his shoulders. "And what makes a nerd anyway? So, you have poor eyesight and like comic books. Big deal! At least you're passionate about something. What's Chad passionate about?"

Nick shrugged.

"Football I guess," he said.

"So, then Chad's a football nerd. What about Marco?"

"Pfft, Marco isn't passionate about anything other than weed and Trixie."

"Then he's a junkie nerd. And look at Conrad. He's clearly a business nerd." Gillian squeezed his shoulder gently. "Just because you like the things that they don't doesn't make *them* any better or *you* any worse. So, yes Nick, you are a nerd, and you should wear that badge with pride."

He looked up from his shoes to see that earnest smile from earlier. He smiled back awkwardly and realised that he was quite fond of his new colleague.

"Also, you're clearly smitten with Lucy," she said as she turned back to her plate and bit into a Twinkie.

The color drained from Nick's face.

"W-what?" he said.

"Oh c'mon, don't give me that," said Gillian. "She said hi and you went all gooey."

"No, I didn't!" Nick balked.

Another *shush* echoed from the receptionist.

"Chill out Casanova," whispered Gillian, "your secret's safe with me. Besides, it's cute."

"What's cute?"

"You are, dummy," said Gillian.

Nick felt his cheeks heating up again and chanced a glance toward Gillian. She turned her attention back to the Twinkie and stared aimlessly around the hall.

Yes, Nick thought, he was definitely growing fond of her.

SEVEN

They returned from lunch fifteen minutes later in significantly better spirits than when they left and all the would-be counselors returned to their seats. Brandon and Lucy sat holding hands while Marco and Trixie stank of stale cigarette smoke with a hint of Marco's favourite substance. The two wore smirks and glassy eyes yet appeared less hostile.

Wallace was sat to the side of the group sipping a party cup of cola that, judging by the odour, was laced with something harder. Conrad was stood with Chad to his side.

"Hope you all had a good lunch," he said. "We won't keep you much longer, however it's important to go over the itinerary for the next couple of days before camp opens.

"And for that, I turn to my right-hand man here, who legitimately has more experience with things over at Camp Summerside than I. So, Chad, I pass the baton to you."

Chad nodded and beamed as Conrad sat down.

"Thank you, Mr Ellis," he said, his voice noticeably deeper than usual. "Just a couple of ground rules before we get started. Firstly, if you have any questions or issues, come to me, ok? And if I'm not around, you can contact Conrad via the onsite radio, but in all instances try to find me first.

"Secondly, no alcohol *at all* on camp grounds. You're all too young to drink anyway but what you get up to in your spare time is none of my business. It *becomes* my business though when you break the law onsite. Same goes for any other substance you may be tempted with." He glared at Marco and Trixie, who offered a smirk and wink. "Smoking in general is advised against, but if you must do it, do it behind the medical hut or out of view of any guests.

"Thirdly, what I say goes. Both Mr Asher and Mr Ellis have entrusted this job to me, and I take it very seriously. You even *think* about rule breaking of any kind and you're gone, no second chances.

"And finally, have fun. While I expect professionalism from all of you, I'd have a major stick up my butt if expected you all to be super serious this summer. The kids are expecting a good time, so you should have one too."

There were smiles from the group, though not with humor. The sheer corniness of Chad's final rule could only have been the words of Wallace Asher.

Trixie raised a hand.

"Yes?" said Chad.

"So, you take your job seriously?" Trixie asked.

"Of course."

"But we don't need to be super serious?"

"I don't expect you to be, no." Chad frowned.

"So, serious, but not *super* serious. That right?" Beside her Marco was sniggering.

"Is there a point to this?" Chad asked.

"No, no point at all. Just wanted to be clear," she said with a victorious smile, although what she had gained victory over was lost on everyone else.

Conrad stood and clapped his hands together.

"Thank you, Chad," he said as Chad sat back down with a face like thunder. "Tomorrow we will head to the camp itself, which I know you're all very excited about. We'll be there for two days ensuring that everything is prepped and ready for the arrival of our campers, so wear comfortable clothes as there'll be a lot of work to do.

"You'll need to be up bright and early; we're meeting down at the docks at 8am."

"The docks?" asked Nick. "We'll be going across the lake?"

Conrad smiled and said, "You are one-hundred percent correct my friend."

Nick clenched a fist and let out a quiet and excited *"Yes"*.

"You won't need to bring too much with you," Conrad continued. "I'll bring lunch for you all and you won't be moving onto camp proper until Friday so no need for suitcases. Tomorrow will simply be about getting to know the camp and checking everything is in working order.

"Any questions?"

The group did not react, looking at one another to see who would speak first. Curious glances were made as nervous smiles were shared.

"No one?" asked Conrad.

Trixie gingerly raised her hand.

"Yes Trixie?"

"So, we can go home now, right?"

Chad rolled his eyes and Conrad could not resist giving a *really?* stare.

"Yes Trixie, that's it for today. Just remember to be at the dock by 8am."

She nodded as she and Marco stood. The rest of the group also stood and offered smiles and thanks to both Conrad and Wallace, who watched as their counselors filed out. Chad hovered briefly until Conrad advised him that he could leave also.

Once the hall was empty, Wallace sighed and reached into his pocket and produced a hip flask, where he unscrewed the lid and took a sip.

"Did you have to put that in your coffee while they were here?" asked Conrad.

"They're kids, they wouldn't care."

Conrad looked at his mentor, sighed, and shook his head.

"You're probably right."

"Marco and Trixie might be a problem," said Wallace.

"Potentially but leave them to me. I've dealt with plenty of punks like that in my time. All it takes is being made an example of and they'll step in line."

"That sounds a bit cruel."

"Oh, it won't be anything terrible," said Conrad, "and they're bound to screw up sooner or later. Besides, having your ass handed to you builds character, especially at that age."

"I don't know. Back in my day wayward youth was rare. You were brought up to respect your elders. Such disrespect would not be tolerated."

Conrad placed a hand on Wallace's shoulder and said, "And it won't be, you have my word. You just have to give them enough rope to hang themselves with."

He checked his watch.

"So, what does Wallace Asher plan to do with the rest of his day?"

"He plans to drink solidly until he falls asleep in front of The Tonight Show." Wallace took another swig from his flask. "Do you need me at all for the rest of the week or do you think you'll be ok?"

"Wallace, this is the beginning of your retirement," said Conrad. "Put your feet up and relax. Unless the emergency flares are used, I'm sure we'll be ok."

Wallace chuckled. Had he known then just how prophetic the younger man's words would be, he would have closed Camp Summerside then and there.

EIGHT

Deputies Pratchett and Foster were sat opposite Sheriff Clark at ten minutes to two and looking none too happy to be there. Doug, as ever, remained outwardly impassive. Internally he was miserable.

He had achieved the impossible and arranged the transfer from Lake Side hospital to Spring Hill Correctional Facility, aided by a county law-clerk who had arrived at the Sheriff's department with the relevant documentation that was signed by the Judge and witnessed by Bob Turner. The sudden appearance of the clerk was enough to tell Doug that the Judge had the foresight to plan the transfer in advance.

"Smoke if you've got 'em boys," the Sheriff said to his deputies. Foster produced a pack of Camels and offered one to Pratchett, who declined.

"Sorry to call you in on your day off," he continued.

"What's this about boss?" asked Pratchett.

SUMMERSIDE LAKE MASSACRE

"I don't know whether you've heard, but we lost the final appeal in the Karl Molyneux case. The judge ruled that there was no further reason to delay transferring him to Spring Hill Correctional."

Foster snorted in disgust.

"Fucker should've gotten the chair," he said.

"Irrespective of what he *should've* got, the law has sided with him. The judge wants him moved *tonight*."

The deputies simply stared.

"That's soon ain't it?" Foster asked.

"Yes, it is," said Clark.

"Can he do that?" asked Pratchett. "I mean, can the judge legally demand that so quickly?"

"The county prosecutor, Clive Barstow, doesn't think so, but that doesn't mean we can ignore it. Tonight, we are moving Karl Molyneux and that's the end of it."

"What time?" Foster said.

"We're efforting that Spring Hill will be ready to receive him by nine-thirty this evening, which means you will need to be at Lake Side for collection by nine."

Clark ran his fingers through his hair and sighed.

"Nothing about this is good boys, and I feel your anger. The Judge is flexing his muscles and we can likely contest this decision in due time but getting this in front of another Judge won't be possible for another day or two. Our Judge isn't totally stupid either. He knows the transfer will cause a stink around town; it's why it's happening so late. So, for now, we must do what we're told.

"I've allocated you a cruiser and you will have shotguns as well as your sidearms. Security will meet you at both facilities and a contingent of armed guards will follow you from Lake Side in a separate vehicle. Rest assured; we will not be taking any chances with this man. He may have fooled the review board and the Judge, but he is still extremely dangerous. Do *not* assume otherwise. Are we clear?"

Both deputies nodded.

"Good. Questions?"

"Yeah, what do you want us to do between now and then?" asked Pratchett.

"I want you to head to archives and read up all about our friend Molyneux. You need to know who you're dealing with."

Foster smiled.

"C'mon Sheriff. Everyone in town knows the stories," he said.

"Believe me boys," said Doug, "the reality is far worse."

NINE

Gillian, Nick, Lucy, and Brandon were sat snuggly in a booth at the local diner, McCoy's, where they waited for milkshakes and cheese fries.

Once Gillian and Nick had left the induction meeting, they stood awkwardly together as they watched Marco and Trixie walk off, Marco's arm slung sleazily over Trixie's shoulder. Trixie did not seem to mind and as he whispered in her ear she gasped and playfully nudged him before placing a hand on his backside.

There were few guesses as to their plans for the rest of the afternoon.

"They're about as subtle as an axe to the face," said Gillian.

"Well, they're having fun I guess," Nick said. He turned to Gillian and rubbed the back of his neck. "So, erm, what you up to now?"

Gillian cocked an eyebrow.

"Well, right now I'm stood talking to you," she said and smirked.

"Oh! I mean, what I meant to say, if you're not busy-"

Gillian punched him lightly on the shoulder and said, "I'm messing with you Nick." She looked at her watch. It was half past two. "I was just gonna head home and watch TV. What do *you* want to do?"

Nick continued to rub the back of his neck as he felt his cheeks flush.

"Well, if you wanted to, I was wondering if you-"

"Hey guys!" came the call from behind them. Both Nick and Gillian turned to see Lucy strolling towards them with Brandon a few steps behind. "What you up to?"

Gillian looked over to Nick with a smile while Nick shuffled his feet.

"I don't know," Gillian said, "but I think Nick was about to have an idea."

"Oh cool!" said Lucy, looking at Nick expectantly.

"Erm, well, I was about to see if Gillian wanted a milkshake."

"That's a great idea!" Lucy beamed. She turned to Brandon and asked, "Fancy a milkshake babe?"

Brandon frowned and said, "I thought we were going to-"

Lucy touched Gillian's shoulder, oblivious to Brandon's protest.

"I know the best place," she said. "Follow me."

The walk was relatively quiet, though not awkward. Whenever there was conversation, it was Lucy that would initiate it. The girl seemed to show genuine interest in Gillian and her life before Summerside Hills. By the time they had reached McCoy's diner, the ladies had linked arms as if they had been friends for years.

Brandon stewed and did not say a word.

The milkshakes were great and the four of them drank in content silence. When they were done Lucy ordered another round as their fries arrived. These were just as delicious.

For Gillian the afternoon was becoming something of a comfort blanket. She had left behind a small but loyal contingent of friends back in Seattle and while they all promised to contact her, the reality for Gillian was that they would drift away soon enough. It was a sad fact but an inevitable one.

In her short time as a resident of Summerside Hills, she had yet to meet anyone she could call a friend. There were plenty of acquaintances, though few were her age. The neighbors were pleasant and showed a friendliness that would have been considered odd or intrusive in Seattle. It was a trope that carried to the town as a whole, where strangers bid you good morning with a genuine smile.

And now it seemed to extend to her fellow counselors.

Lucy and Brandon shared stories of their life at school together, stories that Nick was also privy to. They spoke fondly of school though were clearly ready to move on. Lucy and Brandon had a maturity that was beyond their years. They continued to radiate the same calming aura Gillian had sensed during the induction. It was infectious enough that Nick, sweet, awkward Nick, visibly relaxed.

As the conversation continued, Gillian's gaze fell upon that morning's edition of the *Summerside Gazette* that was on the opposite table. She tilted her head and squinted as she read the headline:

WHAT WILL HAPPEN TO KARL MOLYNEUX?

She reached over and took the newspaper.

"What's happening in the world?" Lucy asked.

"Whose Karl Molyneux?" said Gillian, looking up and pointing to the headline. The front page showed a blown-up version of Molyneux's original mugshot. The man was young, not much older than Conrad, and had a thousand-yard stare that was made more unsettling by the slight upward tilt of his lips in a perverse facsimile of a smile.

"He's a monster, that's who he is." This came from Brandon, who had become very serious.

"Why, what did he do?" asked Gillian.

"He killed a bunch of people back in '59," said Lucy. "They're still not sure what triggered him but when they caught him, he had killed, like, fifteen people, including his wife."

"I heard it was only five?" said Brandon.

"And I thought his wife was still alive?" said Nick

"Fifteen, five, who cares," said Lucy, "he killed a bunch of people and went away to Lake Side hospital for the criminally insane."

Gillian nodded and said, "Does that make him criminally insane? People get killed all the time in the big cities."

"This isn't the big city," said Lucy. "The last time someone was murdered in Summerside Hills was back in 1892 over a card game. And it wasn't just the fact that Molyneux killed them, it was *how* he killed them. That's why he's in the mad house and not prison."

Gillian was enthralled.

"How…how did he kill them?" she asked tentatively.

Lucy quickly looked around the diner. There was no-one sat close, though she still leaned in conspiratorially.

"Well," she said, "I heard he cut someone's balls off."

Gillian's eyes widened.

"No way!" she said.

"That's bullshit," said Brandon. "That's a rumour started by Chad's uncle. I'm sure of it."

"I heard he carved up a kid's face," said Nick, looking terrified. "And then he walked around with the face in his hands like he was carrying a set of car keys or something."

"That's also bullshit," said Brandon. "It wasn't a kid."

"But he still cut up someone's face?" asked Gillian.

"Yeah, that bit is true," said Brandon. "My aunt is a nurse at the hospital. She had to tend to the victims that were still alive and, yeah, this guy was brought in with much of his face missing. Apparently one of the other nurses fainted and the doc on call left the room to vomit. The victim was just visiting a relative, he wasn't even a resident. He did eventually die, although it was blood loss from stab wounds in his abdomen rather than what happened to his face."

Gillian had turned white.

"That's horrible," she said meekly.

Brandon nodded and said, "My dad is the legal clerk for the county. Apparently, there's been some tension in the prosecutor's office and the Sheriff ain't too happy."

"Why's that?" Gillian said.

"Because Molyneux's up for review. As part of his treatment, he's reviewed every five years to see if he's ready to be released or transferred to a more minimal security prison. It's been twenty-five years and my dad says there's a good chance the county may be lenient on him."

"How can your dad possibly know about that?" asked Lucy honestly. "Not to be mean, but he's a clerk. What information can he have possibly seen to know that that's about to happen?"

Brandon shrugged.

"Just an intuition he has I guess," he said.

"Well, *my* intuition says that we stop talking about Karl Molyneux and order some more fries," Lucy said. She pointed at Gillian. "You game?"

Gillian looked at what remained of their last plate, with residual pieces of re-solidifying cheese and spatterings of ketchup and could only think of the anonymous faceless man who had just been in the wrong place and the wrong time.

"I think I'll pass," she said.

"Suit yourself," said Lucy. "Nick?"

"I'm with Gillian on this one," he said, looking pale. He looked at his watch. "Actually, I better get home."

Before Lucy could object, Gillian said, "Me too. My mom will be wondering where I got to, and I need to get ready for tomorrow."

"Ah, c'mon guys," said Lucy. "It's not even five."

Gillian placed ten dollars on the table.

"Sorry. It was nice talking to you though," she said with a genuine smile. "See you bright and early tomorrow?"

Lucy smiled back; any annoyance forgotten.

"Damn straight," she said.

*

He watched the new girl and the geek from the trees across from the diner.

He was barely hidden and at a casual glance he would not appear out of place. He was dressed in the uniform of the Clark family sawmill though he did not work there and never would. The uniform itself was stolen late the day before from the company stores. It was an easy steal; he simply walked in as most were working and grabbed the closest uniform to him. It was a slightly tighter fit that he would have liked but that was fine.

The new girl and the geek talked briefly. The girl appeared aggrieved by something, and the geek was awkwardly attempting to comfort her. The conversation was brief and ended with the girl offering a quick kiss on the cheek before they went their separate ways. The geek walked away beaming.

The scene itself was cute but unfortunate. They were not part of his plan yet would have to die with the others.

He could not afford to let any of them live.

TEN

Wallace Asher was as good as his word and as Johnny Carson made his entrance on the Tonight Show, he sipped at his second neat bourbon of the evening and felt the unmistakable beginnings of drunkenness.

Upon leaving the town hall earlier that day, Wallace had detoured to the nearest liquor store and purchased a bottle of Wild Turkey along with a box of cheap but sizable cigars. As he took them to the till the proprietor, an aging lady of a similar age to Wallace named Cassandra, smirked.

"Party tonight, is it?" she asked with amusement.

"A gift to myself, I'm afraid," he said with a weak smile.

"To yourself?" said Cassandra.

"Yes ma'am. Call it an early retirement present."

Cassandra had looked confused but did not pry further. There was a feeling of melancholy radiating from Wallace that she did not want to press. She had smiled meekly, made a bland congratulatory comment that meant little, and took the fifty dollars Asher was holding. The change was minimal and after Cassandra rung up the purchase, Wallace left the store.

He was surprised by just how miserable he would feel selling the Camp. It had been his life's work and one of the few successful ventures in his professional life. It was a project that had propelled his status within the town, something that had stuck for all the years of the Camp's maintenance and success. His legacy was tied to it. Not that the Camp coming under new management would taint that legacy, but it was his baby. He had nurtured it from an unkempt piece of land to one of the most successful summer programs in the American northwest. Other than the Clark's and young Chad's father, who else in town could attest to that level of prosperity?

Of course, it had all nearly died in that very first year.

Asher had read the news and heard the rumour mill: Molyneux was up for review. While the whole town hated that man, Wallace almost had to thank him. Had that psycho's rampage not been there to distract the town, Wallace's dream of the best summer camp in the region was almost dead before it had even started.

Thank goodness for small favors.

Wallace topped up his bourbon and sighed.

He could not be *too* bitter. He had considered retirement for some time and begun dwelling on it in earnest when Stephen Haig, the Camp's janitor, had broached the subject of his own departure. Conrad's arrival in town had merely expedited the process.

That and his generous monetary incentives.

It seemed odd to Wallace that such a young man would be willing to invest quite so much capital in what was ostensibly a retreat for children. Wallace could not begin to imagine the stress of working in a city like New York. For someone as young as Conrad to make as much money as he had and still move away for sanity's sake told Wallace all he needed to know about that dreadful city.

No, he had nothing to fear in relinquishing his control on Camp Summerside. Conrad was eager but earnest, and compared to the intricacies of the stock exchange, running a summer camp would be a piece of cake.

Wallace continued to sip his bourbon, his mood significantly lifting, when there was a knock at the door. His brow creased as he looked at the clock above his TV. It was approaching midnight.

Who would be knocking at this ungodly hour?

The knock came again, more earnestly.

"Christ," he said to himself. "Gimmie a second!" Wallace placed his whiskey tumbler on the floor by his La-Z-Boy and stood. His brain was foggy from the alcohol and his gait was unsteady.

The knock came again.

"Jesus, I'm coming god-dammit!"

As he clasped the door handle, he inhaled deeply and composed himself.

He opened the door.

"Oh!" he said surprised. "I wasn't expecting to see you here. Is anything the matter?"

His guest stared. It was only then that Wallace noticed he was wearing an ankle long raincoat and leather gloves.

In the guest's right hand was an enormous carving knife.

"What in the hell-"

The guest plunged the knife into Wallace's side.

His eyes widened in shock as he tried to breathe. The whole blade had penetrated the gap between his ribs and pelvis up to the hilt. He could feel the knife's presence in him like a shard of white-hot steel, its heat now blossoming outward as pain began to register. He tried to speak, to ask his attacker why, yet his mouth flopped aimlessly like a goldfish.

The killer pulled the knife free and watched as blood poured from the wound. All strength left Wallace and he buckled, falling to the ground like a ragdoll as his shirt soaked through with blood that was thick and sticky. The smell was appalling and as he looked up at his killer, terror found him and began to scream.

His murderer calmly stepped through the door and closed it gently behind him as Wallace began to crawl backwards, not that he would get far. The amount of blood startled him as it flowed unabated. And the pain, by God the pain. Even the slightest of movements sent spasms through his body, the likes of which he would never wish upon his worst enemy.

The killer stood over him and watched with quiet amusement as his victims' gargled screams continued.

SUMMERSIDE LAKE MASSACRE

The killer held up a finger to lips.

"Be quiet," he said. "No one's coming to help you."

Wallace's screams turned to bitter sobs as his face creased in fear. The killer was right, of course. Wallace's nearest neighbor was a mile away and no amount of screaming would change that fact.

"But why?" he asked, pitifully.

The killer knelt on Wallace's abdomen, sending a fresh wave of agony through him. The scream he issued forth was both miserable and pathetic.

The killer grabbed Wallace by the hair and placed the knife against his neck.

"If you have to ask, you don't deserve to know."

He slid the knife slowly into Wallace's neck and watched with glee as his victims' eyes widened. He thrust the blade upward with sustained force until it slit through the skin at the mandible, through Wallace's tongue, and into his mouth. He continued to watch as Wallace's eyes rolled back in his head and his body slumped. Whether the man was dead or unconscious, the killer did not care, he simply retracted the blade and stabbed at the neck again, and again, and again.

*

The killer exited Wallace Asher's house, his raincoat red with arterial spray.

In his right hand was the bloodied knife, still dripping.

In his left hand he carried Wallace Asher's head by its hair. It would prove useful in the coming days.

PART TWO

THE CAMP

"You're going to Camp Blood, ain't ya? You'll never come back again."

Friday the 13th, 1980

ELEVEN

The tale of Karl Molyneux was as varied and speculative as any piece of modern folk lore. Becoming the archetypal boogeyman to the town of Summerside Hills was a given, yet among the conjecture, there was a very real crime that had shocked not just the local community but the nation too.

Protected from the north by Mount Rainier, Summerside Hills, like so many towns its size, took great pride in its sense of community, and everyone knew everybody else's business.

Before his killing spree, Karl Molyneux was known for his quiet, pleasant demeanor. He worked as a cashier at the local Rosauers and was popular with his customers. This was a trait he extended to his neighbors too, who described him as a friendly, no-nonsense man who loved the company of others as much as he did his wife, Sophia, herself an introverted personality that was rarely seen outside of the company of her husband. A model housewife, Sofia took great pride in her role within the marriage and enjoyed keeping the home perfect for her husband.

There were some who said that Karl seemed at odds with himself; a person who exhibited extroverted traits despite the gentleness in his speech.

As it turned out, the reasons for this dichotomy were appallingly sinister, for Karl certainly was a conflicted man.

In later interviews after his incarceration, Molyneux would admit to having demons from a young age, ones he successfully kept hidden until that fateful night. Where others felt horrified by the despicable aspects of humanity, Karl felt elation. At the age of eleven he felt a perverse satisfaction at coaxing a neighbor's dog out of hiding before stomping it to death. The trust his canine victim showed turning so desperately to fear gave him a high he had never experienced before. During his first sexual encounter, he stated his ability to maintain an erection was based solely on imagining his partner as a mutilated, screaming victim. And when his wife had miscarried, he excused himself to the men's bathroom at Summerside Hospital where he promptly masturbated to the stimulus of Sophia's grief.

Yet through all this time he was intelligent enough to know that such behavior should remain hidden. He built a mask to conceal his true nature and he was good at it too, with his peers respecting his privacy rather than seeing his festering psychopathy.

And for years he remained that way: unseen yet social, the

perfect husband and member of the community.

Then Sophia found his collection.

It was pure chance that took Sophia to their garage that day, to Karl's workbench, a place she had never ventured for their whole five years of marriage. She had never been explicitly told not to rummage around his workstation. In fact, the workbench and its tools were something Sophia had no interest in. DIY and general crafting projects were Karl's hobby and while there had been plenty of times the two of them had shared a beer with her sat on the hood of the car while he worked away at something, the urge to rummage around his space just never took her.

The door to the basement where the Molyneuxs kept their laundry space was proving difficult and creaky to open. Sophia sighed. She had asked Karl repeatedly to fix the hinges. He had yet to do so due to the increased frequency of after work training. Yet, if there was one piece of knowledge she had learned from her husband during all those times watching him work on his projects, it was that Castor Oil was a good lubricant to have to hand. If there was anything that could help her with the basement door, that would be it.

She found herself in the garage on her hands and knees rummaging through the floor cabinet in the storage compartment of Karl's workbench, in a vain attempt to find the oil, when she happened across a cardboard box.

The box itself was nothing more than a tattered old shoebox, yet she reasoned that men, the unorganised and cluttered creatures that they are, were apt to use any old container to store their accumulated junk. It was very possible the item she was looking for was in there.

She opened the box.

There was no Castor Oil.

What there was, was a snapshot into her husband's depraved mind that she never knew existed.

She knew that men liked to gawp at images that were not their wives. It was something she and Karl had spoken about quite honestly before they married. It was Sophia, in fact, that had said: "Of *course* I'm still going to find other people attractive. It doesn't mean I want to be with anyone else though." When she found a copy of Playboy magazine in his bedside drawer, she did not think anything of it.

But what was inside the shoe box went far beyond anything seen in an adult magazine.

There were six neat piles of Polaroids that, to Sophia's eyes, did not appear to be in any discernible order. The photos at the top of each pile depicted acts of fornication that were as sickening as they were grotesque.

She knew men were entitled to their privacy and that certain matters were discussed only in the company of friends, usually with a glass of scotch and a good cigar. They were not conversations she wished to join, nor did she ever think Karl would express an active interest in anything outside their marital bed. Yet, as she looked in horror and took a handful of photos from one of the piles, she realised that Karl's tastes were unlike anything she could have imaged.

SUMMERSIDE LAKE MASSACRE

The pictures depicted the more extreme ends of sadomasochism and the people in the photographs did not appear to be willing participants. She counted five young adults, both male and female, that were naked and bound to wooden benches. There was real fear in their eyes. One captive stared at the camera, her mascara smudged, with welts all over her arms and legs.

The pictures got gradually worse and began to feature the assailants, all of them men. She did not recognise them, though the acts they were performing became more explicit. The welts were clearly the result of blunt force trauma and as the victims' eyes turned more desperate, their attackers' smiles grew larger.

And then, just as her horror reached its peak, Sophia saw her husband.

The photograph in question was not the worst she had seen, though that provided little consolation. Karl was staring at one of the bound young boys who could not have been much more than sixteen, with a smile that chilled Sophia to the bone. It was a look she wished she had never seen nor wished to ever see again. It was not too dissimilar from those warm loving smiles he gave her daily. His eyes, however, were nothing short of terrifying. They were wide with glee and sparkled like a child with a new toy. They did not see a helpless young man. They saw a plaything.

While Karl's left hand rested on a companion's shoulder, his right hand was wrapped around his substantial erection.

"You weren't meant to see those."

Sophia gasped in shock and jumped up, the box of photographs dropping from her lap and scattering the despicable evidence of her husband's transgressions across the garage floor. Karl leaned against the door frame with his hands in his pockets, eyeing his wife with an expression that chilled her to the core.

"Tell me they're not real," Sophia asked him, shaking.

"I could, but it wouldn't be true," he said.

Sophia's bottom lip quivered as the first tear fell. If she had just waited for him to come home, she could have asked him to fix that damned basement door and she would have been none the wiser.

But did she truly want to be ignorant to this? Now that she knew, the fear of what he could be capable of came rushing forth like a burst hydrant.

"When?" she asked.

"When what?"

"When did this happen?" she said pointing to the littered photographs.

Karl shrugged.

"Remember my weekend away in Phoenix?" he said.

She did remember. He had gone for three nights only two months prior, ostensibly for a work conference. It was clear, now, that this was not the case.

"But who were those people?" she asked.

"No one that'd be missed," said Karl casually.

Fear blossomed into anger at the sheer indifference he showed.

"No one that'd be missed?" Sophia said, incredulously, her usual timidity evaporated. "They looked like *kids!*"

Karl shrugged again.

"What do you want me to say?" he asked. "You saw the pictures. It's clear I enjoyed it."

Sophia's face creased with palpable rage. The man of her dreams, the absolute rock in her life and one true love, was a fiction. The real man was a deranged monster, one that was stimulated at the suffering of others, who relished in their misery as a means of gratification.

She did not think. The took the closest thing to hand, a screwdriver, and ran at him.

Karl had anticipated this. As she reached him, the screwdriver held above her head, he struck her hard across the face. She dropped to the floor, out cold, and as she struggled to breathe Karl pulled a weapon from behind his back, a bread knife, knelt beside her limp form, and began sawing it hard against her throat. Sophia regained consciousness, though briefly, and grabbed at the wound in her neck, peering up at the monster that was her husband as he looked on, indifferent.

It took twenty seconds for her to bleed to death, the flow from her wound blooming around her angelic head as she lay still.

Karl stood and tilted his head inquisitively, waiting to feel something, anything, and when nothing came, he turned and made his way to the kitchen. He lit the gas stove, rolled up the morning paper, and rested it on the naked flame. Once it caught, he strolled into the living room and left it to burn away the lie he had been living.

With his wife dead there would be questions asked of him that even the most elaborate of answers would not save him. These questions would follow him no matter where he went, and as he thought more, he realised he did not care.

Sophia's discovery of his secret felt like a release. It would only be a matter of time before the police would come calling.

★

By the time the fire department arrived, Molyneux had already killed his next two victims.

Upon leaving his house, Karl saw that his neighbor, Jay Curtis, was stood on his porch smoking. Karl hated Jay. He thought the man was a pompous and bitter man with a far higher opinion of himself than was warranted. The kind of man that would belittle your own achievements while inflating his own.

For Karl, his murder was a no brainer.

Jay barely had time to register Karl's approach before he was punched in the head at full force. He fell much like Sophia had, then Karl was upon him, taking his head in both hands and pressing his thumbs into Jay's eyes. The man failed to regain consciousness as his eyes popped and fluid oozed from the sockets. Karl stood with bloodied hands as Jay's wife saw him. Upon hearing her gasp, he kicked open the door with enough force for it to slam into her face, breaking her nose. In her daze she offered several feeble pleas against what was coming yet Karl would not be swayed. He took a metal candle holder from a shelf in their hallway, grabbed her by the hair and hit her repeatedly in the face until her skull caved inwards, and even then, he continued. Once he had finished, the candle holder was imbedded in the woman's skull where her face had once been.

He casually walked into their kitchen, his clothing now caked in gore, and stole the largest kitchen knife they had. He then left the house with murder firmly on his mind.

As the sun began to set, Molyneux prowled the streets of Summerside Hills looking for people to kill. Once he was finally stopped by police there were an additional six victims:

There was Bruce Toomey, the town butcher, who had just left work for the day. As Karl stalked toward him, Bruce offered him a smile that quickly disappeared before he was stabbed in the side of the head. He was dead before he hit the floor but that did not stop Karl from stabbing him a further twelve times all over his body.

There was Candice Towell, a woman in her late seventies who happened to witness the tail end of Bruce Toomey's murder. Karl heard her cry in shock and sprinted across the road, where he tackled her to the floor and slashed her throat. Karl then crudely removed parts of her face. He did not keep them as trophies, and they were found discarded next to her corpse.

There was Eddie Jenner, who did not know Karl and was simply walking home to see his wife and kids. Molyneux approached him from behind, covered his mouth and slid the knife into his back. Unlike Bruce Toomey, Karl left Jenner to bleed to death right there on the pavement.

It was Jenner's cries for help that first alerted the authorities to the ongoing spree. By that time Molyneux had killed two more, a young couple walking hand in hand on their way to the movies. The man, Paul Crampton, had his throat slashed and as his date, Annie Richards, screamed in terror, Karl enacted the same violence against her.

His final victim, the one that would cement his reputation as a true monster, was a nine-year-old girl named Cynthia Bateman. She had been approaching Paul Crampton and Annie Richards with a stick of cotton candy in her hand. She was less than twenty feet from them when they were murdered and screamed a shrill, panicked scream that garnered the attention of Karl Molyneux. By this time sirens were close, and the first police cruiser turned into the street where Molyneux and his final victim stood. As the cruiser came to a halt, Karl had already stabbed Cynthia in the neck and calmly watched her die as the cotton candy rolled into the gutter.

He felt the bullet hit his shoulder and collapsed to the curb as a team of deputies swarmed him and beat him unconscious.

★

It was inevitable that his rampage would become legend, a stain on the otherwise pristine history of a town that, until that night, few people had heard of. It put Summerside Hills on the map for entirely the wrong reasons and even after Molyneux was sentenced and the town tried to move on, there were still visitors from miles around eager to take photos of where the grisly crimes took place.

And it was this man, this monster, that twenty-five years later the law deemed was such a model inmate, that he would be relinquished from a secure unit and moved to a minimum-security prison, where he would be pampered for the rest of his life.

TWELVE

R ain began to fall as Deputy Pratchett and Deputy Foster drove to Lake Side hospital to collect Karl Molyneux for his transfer.

They had both spent the preceding hours reading the case file on their charge and were horrified by what they had read. It shocked them both that such a person should be given a more lenient change to their sentence. Molyneux was an intelligent man and it was obvious to anyone, with even a basic understanding of psychopathy, that he had reverted to his friendly personable façade until the day he could manipulate the relevant people into relaxing his sentence.

Now it seemed that time had come.

Before departing, Sheriff Clark had briefed them fully. Security would meet them at the main gate where they would be led to the patient transfer bay. A mixture of doctors and orderlies would lead Molyneux, in handcuffs, outside and place him in the back of their cruiser, where he would be sat with two members of security on either side. When it came time to leave, they would be followed by a second vehicle with two doctors and two additional members of security in case anything should happen through the journey. When they arrived at Spring Hill Correctional Facility, members of security for both institutions would be responsible for removing Karl from the Deputy's charge. Foster and Pratchett would then call the Sheriff's office where Doug Clark would be waiting for them.

In theory, it should be simple.

Pratchett was nervous and in the twenty minutes since leaving the Sheriff's office he had smoked through half a pack of cigarettes. He flicked his current smoke out of the passenger window and lit another.

"Wanna take it easy there pal?" said Foster as he chanced a look at his colleague.

Pratchett inhaled like his life depended on it.

"I'm about to share a car with a monster," he said. "Cut me some slack, ok?"

"I'm not riding you," said Foster. "But you need to calm down, y'hear? He sees how nervous you are, and he'll be all over that like a rash."

Pratchett looked at Foster. His colleague appeared calmed.

"How are you not freakin' out?" Pratchett asked.

"Oh, I am," said Foster. "I knew a lot of the stories about Molyneux were bullshit but still, that man is a stone-cold psychopath. Killin' that girl? You have to be a particular breed of fucked up to do that. But you gotta think, there's the two of us, armed, along with two guys from security, also armed, and a back-up car tailing us, who have enough munitions to form a militia. Add in the fact that our man will be chained within an inch of his life and we're as secure as we can be. He won't be goin' nowhere."

Pratchett threw his latest cigarette out of the window and reached for another one before hesitating. He had three left.

"We're nearly there," said Foster as they approached the turning for Lake Side hospital. Pratchett returned his pack of smokes to his shirt pocket before catching movement out the passenger window. Though the rain was heavy and the road dark, he was certain he saw the shape of a person in a white gown.

"*Shit!*" yelled Foster as he hit the brakes with both feet. Pratchett was thrown forward against his seat belt as the car juddered forward, the tyres finding little purchase on the rain-soaked road. Foster turned the steering wheel hard to the left to avoid whatever it was blocking his way, before the back wheels skidded, sending the rear of the car in the opposite direction to the front. They spun without control before the tyres finally gained traction and the car came to a stop.

The deputies stared ahead, the cruiser facing the opposite direction from which they had come, as the rain drummed down on the vehicle's roof.

Pratchett turned to Foster.

"What the fuck man?" he said.

SUMMERSIDE LAKE MASSACRE

"There was someone in the road," said Foster, his face white with shock.

A palm slammed against the driver's side window causing both deputies to jump. To their surprise and horror, a middle-aged woman in patient robes was stood outside the cruiser looking frightened and soaked to the bone.

Pratchett came out of his shock, undid his seat belt, and exited the car. He drew his sidearm and pointed it over the roof of the cruiser toward the stranger.

"Don't move!" he shouted as he heard Foster fumble for the radio. "Put your hands where I can see them!"

The lady stared at him, her face a picture of terror and confusion.

"He came!" she screamed through the rain, water cascading down her face as she spoke. "Did you see him?"

"Ma'am, place your hands on the roof of the car!"

"The man! He was dressed in black! He spoke to us, from the sky and in our heads! He said he would open the doors and he did! Did you see him?"

"Pratchett!" Foster shouted from inside the cruiser; his finger pointed to the road behind them. Pratchett stared from the woman to the road leading to the hospital to see a cluster of people walking around aimlessly, confused and all wearing hospital gowns.

"Did you see him?!" the woman screamed again.

"This is Deputy Foster to despatch; I need immediate back-up at Lake Side hospital. There are inmates loose, I repeat, inmates are loose. There is no sign of security personnel. I repeat, this is Deputy Foster calling in any units to Lake Si-"

"DID YOU SEE HIM!?"

"Ma'am, for the last time!" yelled Pratchett as thunder crash above him. "Place your hands on the-"

Whatever hit him, did so with enough force to crack the back of his skull and drop him instantly. He was only faintly aware that something had happened before his face connected with the road, breaking his nose and teeth.

The woman let out a fresh howl of fear before turning from the cruiser and running into the surrounding woodland, disappearing into the darkness.

Deputy Foster haphazardly unbuckled his seat belt and reached for the door handle as the attacker brought up his foot and stomped on Pratchett's head. The wet sound of cracking and squelching was distinctly heard by Foster over the wind and rain, and as he reached for his revolver, opening the driver's side door, he saw the attacker duck down behind the car.

"Freeze!" he screamed before bolting along the length of the car and over the trunk after the assailant. As he made it to the other side he was stopped by the shocking tableau before him.

Pratchett was very much dead, his head split open like a ripened watermelon as dark mushy brain matter oozed from the gruesome opening. His attacker was hunched over the corpse, though he did not wear the same gowns as the inmates. This one wore a black and white striped jumpsuit, like a prisoner awaiting transfer.

SUMMERSIDE LAKE MASSACRE

Karl Molyneux looked up and smiled at Foster. He was holding Pratchett's gun.

Foster raised his weapon. Molyneux fired from where he crouched, the bullet striking Foster in his side. The impact turned Foster violently as he also fired, his shot going wide and hitting a nearby tree. As Foster yelled in pain, Molyneux stood, raised his weapon, and fired a second time. The bullet hit Foster in the side of his head, the entry wound blossoming on his temple as the projectile exited the other side, spraying a mist of blood into the rain. His face briefly registered shock before going slack as his knees gave out and his body fell.

Molyneux fired into the corpse until the magazine was empty, the inanimate form buckling lightly with each impact. The radio in the cruiser was frantic as dispatch tried in vain to reach them.

He stepped over to Foster and collected the dead man's pistol, tossing the empty one aside. He stared into the dark recesses of the woods on either side of the road and smiled. He would get a decent head start at least. If he ran now, he could put some distance between himself and Lake Side hospital before dawn.

Tucking the pistol into his waistband, Karl Molyneux began a slow steady jog into the woods, the trees and darkness enveloping him.

THIRTEEN

The morning was bright and warm as the year's camp counselors met at the Summerside Hills dock. When Gillian arrived, she saw that, other than Marco and Trixie, everyone else was present. Conrad was stood talking to the rest of the group as Chad prepared the boat to take them.

It was her first time seeing the dock up close. There were two main jetties against which were moored speedboats and a large cat boat. The boat being prepared for their journey across the lake was familiar: Gillian had seen it sailing on the water, full of tourists.

The main building on the dock consisted of a small office that had room to seat three people. It backed onto a sheet metal building with an array of equipment. There were kayaks, water skis, a deflated banana boat and numerous rubber rings all lined up neatly along the walls. Against the wall that adjoined the office was a large pile of life-jackets that Brandon was sifting through.

Nick spotted Gillian and waved. Gillian waved back. As she approached the group Conrad looked up and smiled.

"Ah, there she is!" Conrad beamed. "Last but certainly not least."

"Oh! Aren't Trixie and Marco meeting us here?" Gillian asked.

Conrad shook his head and said, "Apparently our dear Trixie has a fear of the water. I'm not naïve enough to believe that personally. I suspect that the early hour had something to do with it, but so long as they're at the camp by the time we get started there won't be a problem."

Brandon rounded the corner with a handful of life jackets of different sizes.

"One for everybody Mr Ellis," he said as he placed them on the ground in front of the group.

"We'll be spending the summer together Brandon, you're allowed to call me Conrad."

"Sure, thing Mr Ellis," said Brandon, winking.

Conrad clapped his hands together and smiled.

"Right, well, you all know why you're here. Over the next two days we'll be going over the camp piece by piece to ensure everything's in order. Much of the groundwork has already been done by our dependable caretaker, Stephen Haig, and he will still be on site to help you too. In the meantime, all I ask is that you behave yourselves. The sooner we get everything done, the sooner we can go home for the evening. Any questions?"

The group stood awkwardly and said nothing. Conrad waited a few moments before clapping his hands again.

"Excellent!" he said. "Well then, without further ado, grab yourselves a life jacket and welcome aboard!"

★

The group was quiet as they crossed the lake. Though the noise from the engine was intrusive, Gillian marvelled at just how serene the view was from the water.

Her and Nick were sat on the bench to the rear of the boat and, at Nick's suggestion, they faced the way they had come, watching Summerside Hills grow smaller as they left their small piece of civilisation behind.

"I see why you like it," Gillian said.

"Huh?" asked Nick.

"The lake. It's peaceful."

Nick smiled and nodded.

"They have kayaks at camp," he said. "Maybe one day, when we've got some spare time, we can go out on the water?"

Gillian glanced at him. He appeared nervous but there was hope in those eyes.

"Away from the kids?" she asked.

"Exactly."

Gillian nodded.

"It'd be nice to experience it without that noise," she said, tilting her head at the onboard motor.

"That does kind of detract from the ambience doesn't it?" Nick said.

"The view *is* still great though," said Gillian.

"No engines on a kayak," Nick continued. "Just the sound of birds and the water underneath you."

"Sounds good," said Gillian.

"Is that a yes?"

Gillian linked her arm with his and sat closer.

"I'll think about it," she said, smiling. "If we have time."

★

They arrived at Camp Summerside in good time and were greeted on the main jetty by an older man who appeared to be of similar age as Wallace Asher. He wore a messy and dirt streaked boiler suit and waders and had a Chesterfield cigarette lodged between his lips.

Conrad slowed the boat as they approached the jetty and waved at the old man.

"Hello Mr Haig!" yelled Conrad. "What a beautiful morning it is!"

"That it is, Mr Ellis, that it is," sighed Stephen Haig as he caught the mooring rope thrown to him. The boat gently came to a rest alongside the jetty and as everyone stepped off, Chad took the mooring rope from the aft end and began securing it. Once secure, Conrad beckoned the group off the jetty and into the camp itself.

Gathering them together he said, "Well everybody, here it is. Camp Summerside. Tell me, who out of you has been here as a guest?"

Nick, Lucy, and Brandon raised their hands.

"Excellent. So, I'm assuming the three of you have met Mr Haig before?"

The three of them nodded.

"And you Chad?"

"I know Stephen," Chad said with an air importance

"Well, that leaves young Gillian here," said Conrad. "This is Stephen, our resident caretaker. Been here as long as the camp itself, isn't that right?"

"That's right," said Stephen, with a distinct southern drawl. "Wallace didn't join you?" he asked, frowning.

"From what Wallace told me yesterday, he intends to sleep off a whiskey hangover this morning." Conrad chuckled. "I'll check in on him this evening when we head back to town. But for now," he turned back to the counselors, "I will pass you over to the very capable hands of Mr Haig here."

Stephen nodded and cleared his throat.

"Firstly, welcome. It's always good to see a bunch of fresh faces, though I already know most of you." He looked around the group and locked eyes with Gillian. "Gillian, was it?"

Gillian laughed and rolled her eyes

"I've been told I'm Rebecca's replacement," she said.

"Rebecca?" asked Stephen.

"Rebecca Wheatley," Conrad answered for Gillian. "We

needed someone to fill her space and Gillian applied."

"Ah yes! Miss Wheatley," said Stephen. "I remember her bein' quite the terror when she was a guest here. Well, I'm sure you'll be just fine Gillian. Welcome." Mr Haig looked at the rest of the group and continued, "Very little has changed here durin' my tenure, so things'll probably be familiar to you. The toilets are still cess pools and the electricity is still from generators. We've had some technological updates, don't you worry, but mostly we aim to keep things as much as they were when we first opened."

There was a rumble that grew as Stephen was speaking, and as he finished speaking the rumble evolved into the unmistakable tattoo of a car engine. The group all stared toward the entrance archway as a beaten-up Chevy rounded the corner, its windows down, *Van Halen* blaring from its speakers.

Conrad folded his arms and raised an eyebrow, unimpressed, while Stephen watched in confusion.

The Chevy came to a stop, as did the music and as the passenger door opened, a cigarette butt was flicked from the driver's side window. Marco and Trixie exited the car.

"Pick up that butt son," said Stephen.

Marco pulled his sunglasses down and sneered at the caretaker.

"What was that?" he asked.

"We're in the middle of the woods. A butt is a fire hazard and I've seen forest fires started by much less, so wherever you threw it, go pick it up please."

Marco snorted in derision.

"And if I say no?" he asked.

"If you say no then you turn around, go home and don't come back," said Conrad sternly. "And that'll be after I've made you pick up the butt anyway."

"You can't make me do anything," said Marco.

"No, I can't, but money can be a great incentive. So, you either pick it up and keep your job, or you're fired. It's that simple."

Marco stared at his new boss with daggers as Trixie watched the exchange with thinly veiled apprehension. After a short moment, Marco shrugged, turned to where he had thrown the dead cigarette, searched for a few quick seconds before bending down to pick it up. As he stood, he made a show of placing the offending item in his half-smoked pack of cigarettes and smiled.

"See?" he said. "It's all good." He slung his arm over Trixie's shoulder and approached the group, as if the exchange had not happened.

Conrad maintained eye contact a few moments longer before averting his gaze to Stephen.

"Want to continue?" he asked the caretaker.

Stephen nodded.

"How about a tour?" he said.

FOURTEEN

The scene at Lake Side hospital was anarchy.

Sheriff Clark arrived around the same time Conrad was preparing the boat to take his counselors across the river. The rain had thankfully stopped an hour before and the sun peeked through gaps in the clouds, though this did nothing to alleviate his apprehension.

Pratchett and Foster's cruiser was being tackled on all sides by the forensics team while a couple of blankets were draped over the corpses for a modicum of decency after death. The blankets themselves were soaked from the rain and already sported patches where blood had seeped through.

Doug stared down at the inert forms and bit back his sorrow.

I sent these men to their deaths, he thought.

"Sheriff!"

Doug looked up past the cruiser and toward the hospital where Deputy Elias Ansel was waving. Behind Elias the anarchy was being quelled as multiple cruisers, deputies, and bordering county police hurried to control the scene. Inmates were still being led back into the main building while orderlies and security guards stood with coffees in hand looking tired and shaken.

Sheriff Clark walked over to the Elias and shook his hand.

"Deputy."

"Sheriff," said Ansel, nodding. "Hell of a morning."

"That's putting it mildly," said Clark. "You've taken charge?"

Elias nodded.

"The county boys weren't too happy. We'll probably get some kick back on jurisdiction but for the time being they're keeping themselves busy."

"How many inmates are we missing?"

"Too early to tell Chief. The county boys are rounding them up as we speak, and we've got three large search parties combing the woods for stragglers."

"What about Molyneux?"

Elias looked grave.

"We haven't found him yet."

Shit.

"You've put an alert out?" asked Doug.

"It's already been done, but, Sheriff, if he's missing he'll have one hell of a head start."

It was Doug's turn to look grave.

"Any idea how the this happened?" he sighed.

SUMMERSIDE LAKE MASSACRE

Elias Ansel pulled his notebook from his back pocket and flipped through a few pages.

"It's scattershot and we have some other deputies getting the security tapes, but I think I've got a general picture."

"General's better than nothing," said the Sheriff. "Shoot."

"None of the orderlies or security guards remember a thing. They all seem to be out of it and one of the Docs has stated that he remembers the coffee tasting chalky. I bet you a dime to a dollar we'll find traces of something in the coffee. Sleeping pills is my guess."

"They all drank the coffee?"

"It's the midnight shift boss. Short of shooting yourself with adrenaline, how else you gonna stay up? It was a skeleton crew too, so they're all drinking from the same pot."

"What about the inmates?"

"Considering how close they were to the hospital I'd estimate that their cells hadn't been open long. We found latex smudges on the control panel in the main security office and on the P.A. system. A few of the inmates said they heard a voice telling them all to leave so I'm guessing that was our perp."

"Ok," said Clark, staring off into the woods.

"What are you thinking?"

"I'm just spit balling here, but hear me out, ok?"

Elias nodded.

"On the face of it, some point yesterday someone was able to get into the hospital, drug the night staff without them noticing, and release the locks on all the doors to allow the inmates to walk free. If that wasn't extraordinary enough, it happened to take place the night we planned to move the most dangerous criminal this county has known. That seems like a fantastic coincidence, doesn't it?"

"That it does Sheriff," said Ansel, "Quite fantastic."

"Or…" said Clark, mostly to himself.

"Or?"

Doug stared off into the distance. It was too convenient.

"Sheriff!" called another Deputy who approached Doug and Elias at a trot. He held a clipboard in his hand.

"What is it Deputy…" the Sheriff asked.

"Graham, Deputy Graham sir," he panted. *Jesus,* Doug thought, *he's little more than a kid.*

"What is it son?"

"It's the patient count sir. We have a problem."

"How big a problem?"

"Three patients are missing: Annette Maxwell, Joseph Heagney, and Karl Molyneux."

Doug and Elias shot each other a look.

"You're certain?" asked Doug.

"One-hundred percent," said Graham. "We've counted three times and it comes up the same each time."

The Sheriff exhaled slowly.

"Shit," he muttered. He turned to Elias and said, "Who's heading the county police here?"

"Lieutenant Layton Wiley. He's orchestrating the search parties."

"Is he out with them?"

"Not that I'm aware of. Last I saw he was studying a map by his cruiser on the other side of the hospital."

Doug turned to Graham and said, "Find Lieutenant Wiley for me son. Tell him I need to speak with him urgently."

Graham nodded and ran off, leaving Clark with Ansel. Clark beckoned the Deputy over.

"Walk with me," he said.

They both began walking toward the Sheriff's cruiser.

"We cannot keep this quiet," said the Sheriff. "It's imperative that an APB is dispatched around the state. There's no telling how far ahead Molyneux is and every second he's loose, he's an extreme danger to anyone he crosses. We'll need Lieutenant Wiley with us but be wary. He has a reputation of glory, not justice. In this case stay on his good side and if it comes to any dick swinging call me immediately."

"Sure boss."

As they reached the Sheriff's cruiser, they heard the pattering of footsteps behind them. Both turned to see a scrawny man approaching them. He was tall but gaunt, an intimidating presence if not in stature then by his uncanny resemblance to the undead.

"Sheriff Clark?" the man asked, extending his hand.

Doug took it and shook it earnestly.

"Lieutenant Wiley I presume?"

"Correct. Pleasure to meet you."

"Likewise."

"May I ask what this is about?" asked the Lieutenant. "Not to be a bore, but we're in the middle of a search that requires my full attention."

Doug nodded.

"Then I'll be brief," he said. "We've ascertained that there are three patients that remain unaccounted for. They are Annette Maxwell, Joseph Heagney, and Karl Molyneux. While Maxwell and Heagney need to be found, Molyneux absolutely *must* be the priority. We will need to work in tandem in order to catch him. It's my understanding that Deputy Ansel has already put out an alert, but we need to go state-wide with this. We need to let all local authorities and news channels know and advise the public to be vigilant. I cannot, *cannot,* stress enough just how dangerous having Molyneux loose is to the public."

"I'm aware of his crimes Sheriff," said Wiley, "but surely the other missing inmates require just as much attention?"

Doug turned to Elias.

"Get Graham on the radio. We need the files on Maxwell and Heagney immediately."

The Sheriff continued as Elias leaned into his radio, "I will leave that at your discretion, but, as one professional to another, please take the threat seriously."

"I'm not laughing Sheriff," said Wiley.

"Neither am I so I'm glad to see we're on the same page," Doug ran his fingers through his hair. "I'm thinking roadblocks at twenty-mile intervals and at state lines. Do you agree?"

Wiley nodded.

"That would be sensible, yes," he said.

"Good," said the Sheriff. "Now I'm putting co-ordination with the Sheriff's department in the hands of Deputy Ansel here. He speaks for me and the department so if you have any issues, run them through him."

"You won't be taking charge directly?"

"I would, however there are a number of things I must attend to in town. I'll install a curfew until Molyneux is caught, ensure Molyneux's likeness is sent out around town, that kind of thing. We also have roughly one-hundred and fifty kids arriving in the next forty-eight hours for summer camp, so I will check in with Wallace Asher and see if he can't postpone. But I can assure you that young Elias here is more than capable of working in my place. Unless, of course, you have any issues with this, in which case air them now, because we won't have time to raise them again until Molyneux's caught or in a body bag."

Lieutenant Wiley chewed the inside of his cheek as he mulled the situation over.

"I have no issues Sheriff. My guys will give you their full co-operation."

"As will mine," said Clark.

Wiley nodded and looked at his watch.

"I need to check in with my search parties," he said and walked away. Doug and Elias watched until he rounded the nearest corner.

"He won't be happy," said Elias.

"I don't need him to be happy, I need him to be compliant,"

Doug said.

"He may still be a problem."

"You let me know as soon as he is." Sheriff Clark opened the driver's side door to his cruiser and climbed in.

"Where are you headed?" asked Ansel.

"Wallace Asher's place," he said. "It's on the way into town. See if I can't convince him to call off camp this year."

"Didn't you hear?"

"Hear what?"

"Asher retired," said Elias. "Sold Camp Summerside to a guy from New York. He's calling the shots now."

Doug frowned.

"What's the new guy's name?"

"Beats me. I aged out of camp ten years ago. If you can't find Wallace it might be worth asking David Edwards."

"From *Summerside Gazette*?"

Elias nodded.

"He knows everything," he said with a wry smile. "His son Chad has worked as a counselor at Camp Summerside for the last few years."

Doug sighed.

"I guess I'll need to speak to Edwards anyway. Send out that press release." He scratched the two days of stubble on his chin. "Keep me posted on Wiley. And make those road blocks a priority. If Molyneux so much as sneezes, I want a cruiser on him in ten seconds."

"I'll take care of it, Sheriff."

Doug nodded. He put the cruiser in gear and drove through the main gate and away from Lake Side hospital.

★

Karl Molyneux woke under an old footbridge. Rarely used, it was decrepit and structurally dubious, but it sheltered him from the rest of the night's rain, for which he was thankful.

Rubbing his eyes of sleep, he came out from under his hiding place and stretched. He peered up through the trees as the sun shone through and the birds sang. It was good to be out in the open.

He had no idea where he was, but he smiled none the less. The man dressed in black, the one who had called to the inmates through the hospital's P. A. system, had promised him salvation and he had delivered. He did not know who his saviour was, nor did he particularly care, but he was grateful.

Karl Molyneux, with his newfound sense of freedom, chose a direction and began to walk.

FIFTEEN

After removing their life jackets, Conrad led the counselors to the central structures located around the edge of the main green, which were the medical and administration hut as well as the main hall. Gillian was surprised at how condensed the central hub was if the large map attached to the outside of the medical hut was to be believed, the camp was significantly bigger than she had first thought.

As Chad raised his hand for the counselor's attention, Stephen Haig walked into the hut behind him.

"Ok," said Chad, "listen up. We have a lot to do before our guests arrive so please pay attention. For today we will be putting you in pairs and assigned jobs that *have* to be completed in the next couple of days. No slacking."

Stephen came back out of the hut cradling a handful of maps and three handheld radios. He placed the radios on the ground by his feet before passing the maps to Lucy.

"Take one and pass 'em on," he said to her with a smile.

"These are the maps that we have available for all our guests so don't worry if you lose one," Chad continued, "however we don't want you getting lost while you get your bearings, so do try to keep a hold of them."

Chad pulled a folded piece of paper from his back pocket. "I have here the pairs you will be working with, and the chores assigned to you. Lucy and Brandon?"

The two raised their hands.

"You'll make sure the boat house is cleaned along with the equipment sheds. After that you will go to Hut A and make the beds there. Questions?"

They shook their heads.

"Nick and Gillian?"

Gillian smiled and linked her arm with Nick's.

"You will clean the main hall there," he casually pointed to the giant structure behind them, "make sure we have enough tables and seats stored to accommodate everyone for meals, and ensure the kitchen is clean. You will then go to Hut B and make those beds. That ok with you?"

They both nodded.

"Finally, Marco and Trixie?"

The pair did not react.

"You're on shower and latrine duty."

"Hey, why do we have to clean the shit house?" Trixie complained.

"Because I said so, that's why," answered Chad as Conrad

raised an eyebrow. "Besides, they're always emptied at the end of each season. They won't be full, just dusty."

"It's literally two huts over a couple of huge cess pools," said Marco. "It'll stink."

"Well, get used to it, because that's where everyone will be doing their business this summer, including you. And once you're done giving the latrines a wipe down, you'll head to Hut C and make the beds there. Clear?"

Marco shrugged.

"Whatever," he said, snatching a map from Nick.

Stephen passed the three radios to Lucy, who passed them round.

"You'll have a radio per pair," said Chad. "Tune it to channel five if you want to contact the group, or channel three if you need to speak to either myself or Stephen."

"Hey, wait a minute," said Trixie, "when we're cleaning the shit house, what will you be doing?"

Chad sighed.

"We have a food order arriving today of all our canned goods for the summer. Stephen and I will be making sure that's all in order."

"Why can't we do that?" Trixie continued.

"Because I said you're on shower and latrine duty."

"Why don't we all just calm down huh?" said Conrad, looking at Trixie and Marco. "Fortunately for all of you, Mr Haig has been here a week already making the camp presentable. Just be thankful you're not cutting grass or refuelling the generators, ok? Also, the sooner you get everything done, the sooner we can call it a day."

Conrad looked at his watch and his eyes widened.

"Now, I'm about to be late for a meeting in town. I should be back this afternoon. While I'm gone, both Stephen and Chad are in charge."

Conrad began to stride toward the boat that was still bumping gently against the jetty.

"Behave yourselves why I'm gone ok?" he called back with a wry smile. The group watched as he placed his head and arms through the life jacket, started up the motor, and waved as the boat turned and headed back toward Summerside Hills.

Once the noise of the boat engine dwindled Chad clapped his hands together.

"Right, let's get to work." He held up his radio. "Remember, any issues either channel three or five. Any questions?"

No one answered.

"Excellent. Let's go."

★

As Conrad left Camp Summerside for his meeting, Sheriff Douglas Clark stood on Wallace Asher's doorstep and rang the doorbell.

The house stood alone at the end of a needlessly lengthy driveway that screamed misplaced opulence. Doug had met the man only a handful of times and while he could not fault Asher's enthusiasm, it was obvious to the Sheriff that he had a higher opinion of his success than those around him. Wallace was a small-town celebrity, nothing more, a fact that had failed to register with him.

Doug tapped his foot and rang the bell a second time.

Within the house the shrill noise sounded through the premises but garnered no reaction. Wallace's headless corpse, obscured from Doug's view, rested where his killer had left it, the blood from the neck having already begun turning brown as it coagulated. Flies had already started gathering.

Had it not rained in the night before, the Sheriff would have seen gruesome footprints on the porch. The rain, however, had washed away all traces of blood outside Asher's house.

Doug sighed. Either Asher was sleeping in or was already on his daily errands. Either way, he was not answering.

The Sheriff looked at his watch and decided to leave Wallace for now. In the interim he would head into town and speak with David Edwards at the *Summerside Gazette*.

SIXTEEN

Chad and Stephen entered the medical hut after handing the counselors their itineraries and sending them on their way. The interior space was small, consisting of an infirmary that had a single bed and a wall mounted first aid kit. To the right of the entrance was an enclosed office, itself minimal, sporting a single oak desk and a three-drawer filing cabinet that was old and dented. Behind the desk was a small, dirty window that only allowed a modicum of light to come through. Additional lighting was given by the bare lightbulb that hung limply from the ceiling.

There were two modes of communication with the outside world should the need arise: a single wall mounted telephone that was left to the hut's entrance, and the DB radio that sat on its own small table opposite the desk. For Stephen, there had only ever been two instances in the camp's history that he could remember needing to call for an emergency.

The telephone was the latest addition to the sparce electrical items at the camp. At Wallace's insistence, the camp had no other electrical luxuries. There were no TVs and no refrigeration: the camp relied entirely on canned or dry produce for food.

Stephen took the telephone off the cradle and pressed it to his ear. He was met with the familiar drone of an open line. In the office Chad turned on the radio and was met with static. He would perform the scheduled radio test at five that evening but everything appeared in order.

The young man sat behind the desk and leaned back in the chair as Stephen stood in the office doorway.

"You know, there's a bottle of scotch in the bottom drawer of that desk," Stephen said.

Chad reached down and pulled but the drawer wouldn't open.

"It's jammed," he said.

Stephen pulled a large set of keys from his pocket and found the one he wanted.

"It's locked," said Haig, smiling. "Can't have it disappearin' on me now."

Chad frowned and said, "Then why tell me about it?"

"I wondered that," Stephen said, "but, between you 'an me, this'll likely be my last year workin' here, so I figured I'd get somethin' special. I'll need someone to toast with though and Conrad told me he don't drink, so I guess it falls to you."

"I'm more of a beer man personally."

"And underage by the looks of you."

Chad smiled.

"I'm twenty-one in two weeks as it happens," he said.

"Well, ain't that mighty fortuitous," said Stephen.

"You don't strike me as the kind of guy to give a rat's ass about underage drinking anyway."

"True enough." Stephen leaned against the doorframe. "What do you make of this year's lot? Know 'em from school?"

"They were all a couple of grades below me. Marco was always a punk, has a chip on his shoulder about life. Trixie *thinks* she's a punk, but she'll fall at the first sign of trouble. I know people like her. They like bad boys until they get one."

"I'll keep that in mind," said Stephen. "The other girl and her fella seem nice though."

"Lucy? She's fine enough. Not a bad bone in her from what I hear. Brandon follows her around like a lost puppy. They'll get married have a bunch of kids and grow to hate each other."

"Cynical."

Chad shrugged.

"Always happens with high-school sweethearts," he said. "You'll see."

"I'll've probably shuffled off this mortal coil by then but I'll take your word for it," Stephen said as he pulled his packet of Chesterfields from his shirt pocket and lit one. He offered the pack to Chad, who politely refused. "Speaking of lost puppies, I think that Nick kid is taken with the new girl."

Chad rolled his eyes.

"What?" asked Stephen.

"You're as bad as a teenager you know," said Chad. "Planning on sharing all the gossip with your girlfriends?"

Cigarette smoke billowed from Stephen's nostrils as he chuckled.

"That's me, queen bee 'n' all that," he said. "I think it's sweet. When you get to my age you find yourself pining for the carefree days of your youth."

"Is that so?"

Stephen nodded.

"Look at it this way," he said. "I'm in my mid-sixties, never taken care of myself, prob'ly smoked a million cigarettes, and spent my entire adult life workin' as a caretaker. I've seen plenty of kids work here in my time and they all have dreams. Life hasn't kicked 'em in the head yet."

"How touching," Chad said, bored.

Stephen scowled at the younger man.

"Ok then," he said. "What about you?"

"What about me?"

"This is your third year doin' this job. I know for a fact you still get an allowance from your parents," Chad began to protest but Stephen silenced him with a wave of his hand. "I heard you talkin' about it to that Britney girl last year, so either you were lyin' or it's true. Don't matter to me. But what you get is a kid who ain't really a kid no more whose parents still front him cash, whose never left his hometown, and who works the summer at a camp that wouldn't even feature in the top twenty best in the country. What you afraid of champ?"

Chad's face gave away nothing, but he fidgeted in his chair.

"Afraid? Who said I'm afraid?"

"C'mon, don't gimmie that," Haig said. "You're not stupid. I don't even think you wanna be the alpha, even though you want folks to *think* you are." Chad began to protest again but Stephen cut him off. "I'm not judgin' and I mean no offense. But you must admit, with who your father is, with the money your family has, you can literally do anythin' you want. So why you still here?"

Chad shrugged and said, "Maybe this is what I want?"

Stephen nodded.

"Maybe it is and maybe when you reach my age you'll look back at your life and have no regrets. But I see how you are with the other counselors."

"What, this group?"

"I mean in general, with this year's, last year's, and the year before that. You strut, sure, especially when there's a pretty girl nearby, but you don't throw your weight around either. They seem to listen to you, same with the kids when they get here."

"And?"

"*And*, it means you have a commandin' presence. Didn't anyone ever tell you that's the making of a manager right there? What's stoppin' you findin' a regular type job that you can make a career from?" Stephen lit another cigarette with his previous one and stubbed the dud in the glass ashtray on the desk.

"Can I bum one of those?" asked Chad.

Stephen nodded and held out the pack of Chesterfields. Chad took one and leaned forward as Haig lit the tip.

Chad inhaled deeply and leant back in the chair as he exhaled the blue smoke. He stared at the ceiling and allowed the silence between the two of them to grow.

"You know what?" he eventually asked.

"What?" asked Haig in return.

"I'm not exactly the biggest fan of my father."

"Hate to break it to you kid, but few people are."

"Ok, so imagine what it's like being his son," Chad said, still staring at the ceiling. "We're not exactly close, even though I live in the same house as him and my mother. He's a believer in tough love but in truth he's a bully. He's rude, belittling, self-aggrandizing, and squashes anyone's achievements so *his* appear better."

"So, he's an asshole," said Stephen bluntly.

"For sure," said Chad. "So, you ask why I'm doing this instead of becoming a CEO or something? Because anything else is out of reach. I'm approaching twenty-one, and all I've been told in life is that I'll never be anything. So, I figure I'll take this job, right? Turns out I quite like it. Turns out I'm pretty good at it, and people treat me well. My Pa, on the other hand, doubles down, tells me I can't even do *this* job properly, that I'm wasting my time, and blah, blah, blah. Like I said, he's belittling, and this *one* thing I can hold up and say 'hey, that's mine' is immediately played down because it isn't his."

He took a long hit of his smoke and continued speaking.

SUMMERSIDE LAKE MASSACRE

"And you know what the worst of it is? It's that damn allowance. He holds it over me like a fucking axe, you know? As soon as I even think about moving onto anything better, it's gone. And it's a good allowance too, better than what I'd make earning three bucks an hour at Rosauers, and that's the point, it's a choice: stay comfortable, but worthless, or leave, make a go at things, but be cut off. And I know that if I do the latter and fail, he won't let me come back home. It's either his way or the highway."

"So, you'd rather be miserable? Is that it?" asked Stephen.

"I'd rather be comfortable."

"Comfortable doesn't mean happy though." Haig lit another smoke and left the pack on the desk. "Help yourself."

"Thanks," Chad said, reaching for another as he stubbed out his first.

"So, you're afraid of failin'," Stephen observed.

Chad shrugged.

"Maybe," he said. "But when I'm here I try not to think about it."

"That's one way of dealin' with it I guess," said Stephen. "However, if I may impart some wisdom, stickin' your head in the sand and hopin' everythin'll be ok isn't the way forward."

"Oh yeah?" Chad said, defensively. "And what would you do?"

"Me? I'd bite the bullet. Screw the old man." Chad looked at Haig with pronounced cynicism. "Don't look at me like that," said Stephen. "Why is that such a crazy prospect? Why do you feel you have to prove somethin' to him? You could be President and he'd still be a shit. If you try and spend your life aspirin' for his validation, then you'll be exactly what he says you are: a failure."

Chad held his gaze for a moment before standing and putting out his smoke and picking up the pack from the desk.

"I'm taking these," he said.

Stephen chuckled.

"Be my guest," he said, "I'm not short on 'em."

Chad placed the packet in his pocket and strolled toward the door. As he brushed past Haig, the older man grabbed him by the arm.

"Seriously Chad: fuck him."

The Lead Counselor gave Haig a nod before shrugging his arm off and walking from the hut.

SEVENTEEN

From outside, the home of the *Summerside Gazette* was as non-descript as any other grey office you would find in any town. It was, however, a ruse. Those that worked within the building, led by David Edwards, wielded significant power over the residents of Summerside Hills and held onto their fiefdom like a guillotine ready to fall.

Douglas Clark had never met David Edwards, which was either fortuitous or deliberate, for the editor's reputation around town was toxic. He was an intelligent man, but a spiteful one, and many knew better than to cross him. He had and eloquent way with words. It was always what was *not* said in print that did the damage.

David Edwards was a snake. Pure and simple.

The Sheriff would have to tread carefully.

He entered the building and was greeted by a small and cold reception area. The walls, once white, were now yellowing from years of cigarette smoke, and adorned with framed pages of the paper's most successful stories. The pages themselves had also deteriorated with age to the point where a light breeze would cause them to crumble.

Behind the desk was a young woman with enormous permed light brown hair, her face buried in a magazine. Douglas cleared his throat. The woman peered over her magazine and smiled.

"Good morning!" she beamed. "How may I help you?"

"I need to speak with David Edwards urgently."

The lady's smile disappeared.

"He's very busy at present. I can schedule you in tomorrow? Would that work?"

Doug walked casually over to the desk and gave a warm smile.

"I really need to see him," said the Sheriff. "Please call him and tell him Sheriff Douglas Clark needs to speak to him as a matter of high importance. Tell him there's a scoop in it for him if he can find the time to meet me in the next ten minutes."

The receptionist blushed and her smile returned.

"Let me get right on that for you," she said.

Doug nodded and as the receptionist lifted the phone he took a seat.

★

Nick and Gillian completed their clean of the kitchen within half an hour and grabbed a couple of warm sodas before moving into the main hall. Barely a word had been spoken between them, though Gillian was pleasantly surprised by how comfortable the silence was. She was happy with Nick, she realised, and was happy to have found a friend for the summer. Being around him was easy and with few friends in the area, that was all she could ask for.

They stood together, looking around the main hall as they gulped their sodas. The hall was huge, easily able to accommodate the one hundred and fifty guests they were expecting. The entrance was dominated by two large solid mahogany doors that were stained with the handprints of hundreds of happy campers. At the opposite end of the hall was a stage that was elevated from the floor by half a metre. Nick grimaced, remembering having to act in an embarrassing play seven years before. There was a small door to the left corner of the stage that lead to a cluttered storage room. The left wall was decorated with a vibrant mural dedicated to Summer Lake, beneath which was a line of framed photographs.

Gillian and Nick leant against the large serving hatch that separated the kitchen from the hall.

Nick wiped sweat off his brow, exhaled and took a drink of his soda.

"You ok?" asked Gillian.

"Yeah, fine. I just get out of puff easily."

"Out of puff?" Gillian said, smiling.

"Yeah," he caught her looking at him and flushed. "What?"

"Nothing, just a cute saying."

Gillian nudged him with her arm and walked to the wall of photographs. The images were much the same, only the faces changed. Each one featured a group of smiling camp counselors stood at the entrance to Camp Summerside, with Wallace Asher stood in the middle of the group. The years were embossed at the base of the frames.

Gillian frowned.

"That's not right."

"What's that?" Nick said as he approached.

"I thought this year was the camp's twenty-fifth anniversary?" she said.

"It is. Why do you ask?"

"There's only twenty-three photos here. Surely there should be twenty-four, not including this year?"

Nick also frowned and looked at the first picture. True enough the date was marked as 1960.

"Odd," he said. "Why isn't there one for 1959?"

"Looks like there was one," said Gillian, pointing to the empty space next to it. The bright sun glaring through the high windows had faded the painted wood over the year, however a darker square remained next to the 1960 photograph.

"That's odd," said Nick. "I've never noticed. I wonder why it was taken down?"

"Who knows," said Gillian. "Some of the others have got nicks and scratches so maybe this one got busted somehow. I'll mention it to Conrad when he's back, see if he knows." Gillian pulled out the list of chores from her back pocket and studied it.

SUMMERSIDE LAKE MASSACRE

"Not much to do in here, just sweep the floor, make sure nothing's fallen in the storage cupboard, and do a count of the tables and chairs."

"Do you really think someone would steal chairs?" asked Nick

"No," Gillian said, "but I'm nothing if not thorough. Plus, the longer we can put off making beds the better. I hate laundry duty, don't you?"

"It's still gotta get done though."

"Yeah, I know," she said, sullenly. "But counting chairs is *sooo* much more fun."

*

David Edwards kept the Sheriff waiting for fifteen minutes. When he finally arrived in reception, he was exactly how Doug imagined him to be.

Edwards emulated the appearance of a Wall Street yuppie yet did not appear to have the money to maintain the illusion. His suit, much like Clive Barstow's, had seen better days. The cuffs appeared worn and there was no discernible crease in his pants. His shirt was unbuttoned to excess, and a tuft of thick brown chest hair bloomed from the opening. His hair was slick, and he was clean shaven, something Barstow could not boast, but the veneer of wealth and power was showing signs of cracking.

It appeared to Clark that Edwards was afflicted with the same bug that plagued Wallace Asher: small-town celebrity with delusions of grandeur.

Edwards smiled and extended his hand.

"Morning Sheriff," he said, taking Doug's hand in a needlessly firm grip. "Sorry to have kept you, we were busy finalising our main story for this evening's edition."

"Not a problem," said Doug, "though it's the evening edition I'm here to discuss with you."

Edwards tilted his head in curiosity.

"Is that so?" he asked with a wry smile.

Doug nodded and said, "Though I would prefer it if we spoke in private. Do you have somewhere we can talk?"

"Of course, we'll head to my office." Edwards turned to the receptionist. "Tiffany, hold my calls, will you?"

"Sure boss," she said smiling.

Edwards led Doug to an office that was little more than an oversized broom cupboard and just as cluttered, though it would do for their purposes. A cloud of tobacco smoke filled the room, and the sheer amount of paper, which covered Edward's desk, presented a significant fire hazard.

The Editor and Chief and The Sheriff both sat, and EdwardS immediately grabbed the cheap cigar that was sat smouldering in the ash tray and began puffing.

"So, Doug," David said, "you're wanting us to sit on our story? Is that right?"

Doug frowned.

"Excuse me?"

"I mean, it's fairly ballsy for Judge Atwell to send the law but

I think you'll find I'm protected under the constitution when it comes to free speech and freedom of the press."

Doug shrugged.

"I literally have no idea what you're talking about," he said. "You have a story on Judge Atwell?"

David smiled.

"Very interesting," he said.

"What is?"

"You honestly have no idea what I'm referring to, do you?" asked Edwards.

"Considering your track record for litigious articles, I'm certain you will have investigated your story to the fullest credibility before going after our county's Judge."

Edward's smile faltered.

"I'm sure I can get my team to look over the story before it goes to print."

"Good man," said Doug. "Frankly, Judge Atwell is on my shit list at present, but as The Sheriff, I advise to be totally correct about *anything* in your story before going to print. Atwell is not known for his sparkling bedside manner."

"I appreciate the warning," said Edwards.

"Well, that one's for free. But I'm really not here regarding that. I *do* need you to hold on it for a day or two though."

"Something more pressing is there?" said Edwards with thinly concealed sarcasm.

"As a matter of fact, there is," said the Sheriff.

David Edwards leaned back in his chair and inhaled from his

pipe.

"Waiting on you Sheriff," he said with an eyebrow raised.

Doug exhaled.

"Karl Molyneux escaped from Lake Side hospital last night."

Edwards' face dropped.

"You're fucking with me?"

"I wish I was," Clark continued. "He killed two of my deputies before disappearing. We have most of the Sheriff's department and county police searching for him but, frankly, he could be anywhere by now. I need you to print a front-page story, with his mugshot, with a strong emphasis on how dangerous he is."

"Armed?" asked Edwards as he learned forward and began taking notes.

"We assume so, yes. We will be placing a curfew for 9pm until he his caught, roadblocks at county lines, and strongly advising anyone to call the authorities should they see him."

"You'll get a lot of crank calls."

"Probably yes, but we'll take any leads."

Edwards placed his pen on his desk and leaned back again in his chair. Clark did not like the smug expression.

"What?" the Sheriff asked.

"Oh, I'm just wondering how the worst spree killer for the last decade managed to escape on your watch, Sheriff."

"You can wonder all you want," said Doug. "It's still very much an active investigation."

"I'm sure it is, but there's going to be a lot of wild speculation once I print the story."

"And?" said Doug.

"And," Edwards replied, "unless I have something a little more concrete, who's to say what assumptions will be made? You're asking to sit on an already explosive story for this. How the Sheriff's department looks when we go to print will ultimately fall to you."

There it was. The snake had arrived. Doug was not surprised though he could not help his anger. Two men had died and here was David Edwards, extorting information.

"I'm sure the deputies that died last night would appreciate a smear campaign from their local paper," he said through a clenched jaw.

"Now don't get paranoid Doug," Edwards said, chuckling, "I'm simply saying I can't go to print with such a slim story."

"It's Karl Molyneux. Surely that's enough."

"His crimes happened a long time ago," Edwards said. "I find it difficult to believe that his name alone carries the same weight as it once did."

It would be pointless arguing with him, Doug realised. He would publish a story that did away with the facts swiftly to make way for wild conjecture that would question the competency of the police. It was a game Edwards was adept at.

Unless.

"What's your story on Judge Atwell?" Doug asked.

Edwards frowned.

"Why?"

"Like I said, he's on my shit list, and if you're about print something that potentially incriminates him in something criminal, I'd like to know."

"I'm sure you would," Edwards said, "but I'm protected under the-"

"Constitution, and freedom of the press. So you keep saying. But if you *are* sitting on something with criminal implications that you refuse to disclose to the police, then that's obstructing a criminal investigation."

Edwards scoffed and said, "As far as I'm aware, there is no investigation."

"Sure there is," Doug said smiling. "It started as soon as you mentioned the story."

Edwards stared at the Sheriff over his cigar.

"You know what?" he said. "Come to think of it, I don't think there is a story. I must've gotten confused."

"Well, you won't mind me using your phone to request a warrant then, would you? Should only take twenty minutes and I can wait here while it's being processed," said Doug. He stood and reached for the receiver.

"Ok! Ok!" shouted Edwards as he placed a protective hand over the telephone. "I'll play. You want the goods on Atwell? Fine. But you get copies of our research and we still run the story tomorrow."

Doug nodded.

"But you don't get any of that unless you give me a little something on the Molyneux case," Edwards continued. "I've got bupkis here."

"Ok," said Doug. "All I can say is that there was definitely foul play involved."

"No shit. Can you be more specific?"

"Early toxicology reports suggest staff and security personnel were drugged."

Edwards scribbled a note.

"Anything else?"

"There were two others that escaped: Annette Maxwell and Joseph Heagney. I'll get a Deputy to send over their mugshots too."

"That's it?"

"That's it. I have literally given you all I know at present."

"I don't believe you," said Edwards.

"I don't care," said Doug. "But how about this? When this is all over, you get an interview with me."

Edwards pondered.

"About the escape?" he asked.

"It can be about when I lost my virginity for all I care," said Doug tersely. "But I know you've been dying to get one on me so, in exchange for the Atwell story, I offer you a no holds barred interview with the town's Sheriff."

Edwards nodded briefly before lodging his cigar back in his mouth and standing.

"I think we have a deal Sheriff Clark," he beamed as he held out his hand. Doug stood and took the editor's hand in a firm shake, before turning to the door.

"Oh, before I forget," said the Sheriff, "The man Wallace Asher sold Camp Summerside to. Who is he?"

"Conrad?" said Edwards. "Young business type from New York. Owned a firm that dealt with mergers and acquisitions, I think. Why do you ask?"

"Conrad who?"

"Ellis."

Doug frowned.

"Why buy a summer camp?" he asked.

Edwards shrugged and said, "Hey, to each his own I say. Now, if there's nothing else, please get the hell out of my office."

Clark did not hesitate and left the office and its resident parasite behind.

EIGHTEEN

To Deputy Elias Ansel's surprise, Lieutenant Wiley proved to be a collaborative partner and while Ansel was busy gathering more information from the orderlies on the events of the previous night, Wiley kept him updated on the progress of their search. While there was no sign of Molyneux, Joseph Heagney's wrist band had been found along with a set of footprints that led toward the river. Wiley had the canine unit already in play and was confident they would find Heagney and Annette Maxwell soon.

Ansel headed to his cruiser and radioed the Sheriff with the news. Though Doug seemed happy, he was clearly distracted so Ansel let him be.

As he took a sip from a cold cup of coffee, there was the distant crack of two gunshots followed by shouting. The commotion was not close, and the surrounding trees made it almost impossible to determine the location. The yelling came to a noticeable crescendo before a flurry of gun fire rained down for a few long seconds.

The proceeding silence was chilling. The small group of officers remaining at the hospital all looked to Ansel for guidance.

"Deputy Ansel?" came the distorted voice from his car radio. It was not a voice he knew. One of Wiley's men.

"Ansel here," he said. "What the hell was that?"

"We found Heagney."

*

Lieutenant Wiley calmly approached the scene of the shooting. His officers surrounded the area, some still in the process of holstering their weapons.

Heagney was on his back and riddled with bullets. He had partially fallen in the river and the blood pooling beneath him began to mix with the running water. He was dressed only in his hospital gown. It had twisted up enough to expose his genitals.

"Cover him up, will you?" Wiley said to no one in particular. One of the officers stepped forward and, taking great pains to avoid stepping in his blood, pulled the gown down enough to cover his modesty.

"Anyone want to tell me what happened?" asked Wiley, still staring at the corpse, his hands in his pockets.

According to the officers, two warning shots were fired as Joseph Heagney attempted to run. He was frightened and abruptly turned to the officers chasing him and made to hold his hands up. This motion was enough to trigger three officers, who opened fire until their revolvers were empty.

Wiley nodded.

"So, it was self-defence?" he asked.

The officer next to him, a new kid by the name of Jackson, frowned.

"Self-defence?" he asked.

"He came at you," continued Wiley. "That's why he was shot."

"But he didn't sir," said Jackson.

"Mills!" Wiley shouted. A short, stout officer in his early twenties appeared next to him.

"Sir?" said Mills.

"See that rock over there?" asked Wiley as he pointed to a fist sized rock by Heagney's feet. It was quickly being encroached upon by the expanding pool of blood.

"Yes sir," Mills said.

"He came at you with that, did he not?"

Wiley stared at Mills with intent. Mills got the message.

"He did," he said.

"See," Wiley said, looking at Jackson. "Self-defence."

Jackson nodded, uneasy. He knew better that to argue with the lieutenant. Wiley cared little.

"Someone bag him up," the Lieutenant said as he turned and headed back to his cruiser.

NINETEEN

L ucy and Brandon got the boat house cleared within an hour and took a quick break to admire the scenery. The camp was beautiful, there was no question, and it seemed absurd to both that they should be paid to be there for the summer.

As they sat on a rickety picnic bench, Lucy linked her arm with her boyfriend's and heaved a contented sigh.

"It's great, isn't it," Brandon said in response.

"No complaints here," said Lucy. She gazed up at him and kissed him lightly on the cheek. He smiled.

"You know, we don't have to take a break before starting college," Brandon said.

"You want to go to college this year?" Lucy asked.

"No, I mean we could just take an indefinite break," he said. "We could see the world for a bit, explore. We might find somewhere to settle, you know, that isn't Summerside Hills."

SUMMERSIDE LAKE MASSACRE

Oh Brandon, Lucy thought and sighed again, but not with contentment. He was prone to flights of fancy, and while most were cute, there were many that were just unrealistic. Of course, the idea of disappearing on their own was wonderful, but where would it leave them in a years' time? Sure, they had thought about travelling, but then what? A high school diploma was fine, but college would open an excess of opportunities that would otherwise be out of reach in their small town.

She looked up at him and caught him staring out at the lake. The sun glinted off the water, bringing out the blue in his eyes. Sweet, wonderful, naïve Brandon. He would understand eventually.

He noticed her looking at him.

"What is it?" he asked.

"Nothing," Lucy smiled. She nodded to the equipment shed fifty feet from the boat house. "C'mon, the sooner we do the inventory, the sooner we can finish."

"But we have the bedding to do too."

"Exactly, so giddy-up Mr." Lucy pecked him again on the cheek and stood. Brandon watched her walk toward the shed and frowned.

There were times he thought his girlfriend did not take him seriously enough. He would mention things in the hope she would engage with them, discuss their validity or show an interest in what he had to say. Her usual response, however, was dismissal. It was a trait that bugged him.

He stood and followed, quietly annoyed with his girlfriend.

★

"Fucking bullshit."

Trixie closed her eyes and kept her cool. They had nearly finished cleaning the latrines, yet Marco had not stop complaining.

They had opted to clean the latrine block before the showers, or rather it was Trixie who had suggested it. It was the worst job, therefore, better to do it first. Marco had agreed but it did not stop his angst, and for the duration of their work they had barely spoken, save for the odd outburst from him.

Telling him to relax was out of the question. Early in their relationship Trixie had spoken back to him in an argument, one that he had started no less, only for him to back hand her across the face. She had barely registered the pain in her jaw when he forcefully grabbed her arm and screamed in her face. The fury she had seen that day truly frightened her and was the first of many moments that emphasised just how grave an error she had made in taking Marco as her boyfriend.

Trixie was angry at herself more than anyone. Being an outcast in school had not been easy and all she had wanted was a modicum of friendship. Marco had approached her at lunch only a year before, with Nick hovering behind, and introduced himself. In hindsight, the red flags were already there. Marco treated Nick poorly, unlike any friend should at least, but Trixie did not care that day, not for Nick at least. Why would she when the hot bad boy was interested in her?

It was not long before Trixie realised, however, that Marco

had seen her as an easy target, one that was surprisingly easy to groom.

She had done things for him she never would have thought where in her before their meeting. She hooked up with him in the backseat of his beaten old car before she knew it and it was not the gentle romantic first time she had always pictured. She had allowed herself to act as a honey trap on more than one occasion, leading easy prey into an adjacent alley only for Marco to knock them unconscious and steal everything they had on them.

And the drugs, she thought, *don't forget the drugs.*

Before meeting Marco, the only substances of note she had tried were the occasional beer she had stolen from her dad's supply – she knew he would never notice - or a smoke as she walked to and from school. Since Marco, there had been vodka, and more pot than she cared admit. It was the pot she actively encouraged him to use. It was a drug she found she quite enjoyed using and when Marco was stoned, he became a much better person to be around. In fact, there was a flattened but intact joint in her back pocket that she planned to break out once they had finished their chores. It would at least calm him down after his anger of the day.

It seemed apparent she may need to break it out sooner.

*

Stephen checked another item off his inventory. In the locked drawer of the office desk, there was not only the bottle of scotch he had shown Chad but also a metal lock box that usually lived next to the radio.

He opened the box to find the items as he had left them last summer: a loaded, bright orange flare gun with a spare flare tucked next to it.

Chad, like every head counselor before him, knew of the gun and its purpose. In the summer of 1972, a counselor had drowned on the lake in a terrible accident. In the aftermath Wallace had opted to include the flare gun as part of their emergency arsenal. Should there be any delays in getting the police on the radio, it was ruled that a counselor would fire the flare gun while contact was being made. Asher had run it by then Sheriff Wydell, who had promised that someone would always be on the lookout should the flare be used. In reality, he had simply briefed his deputies to be extra vigilant.

He opened the gun, removed the chambered flare, and tested the firing mechanism. It still appeared to work. He reloaded the flare, placed the gun back in the box and closed the lid.

From outside he heard the sound of a lorry pulling up. Stephen set the flare gun box next to the radio and exited the hut, where he saw Chad directing the lorry toward the kitchen entrance of the main hall.

He clapped the boy on the shoulder. Chad jumped.

"Jeeze, you gave me a heart attack," he said.

"Sorry," said Stephen. "I'm going to take a look around, see how the others are getting on. You good here?"

SUMMERSIDE LAKE MASSACRE

Chad waved a hand dismissively. Stephen nodded and headed in the direction of the latrine and shower blocks. It would be good to check on their resident troublemakers first.

★

Gillian was two steps behind Nick as they headed to their assigned hut and the mountain of linen that awaited them when they heard the rustling in woods to their right.

It was not uncommon to hear movement of course, as the woods were rife with elk and the occasional owl, however this rustling was sudden and accompanied by heavy breathing.

The two stopped dead and peered into the trees in the direction of the noise.

"What the hell was that?" whispered Nick.

Gillian shook her head.

"One of the guys maybe?" she asked, matching his volume.

"Maybe," said Nick. "Chad?" His voice was suddenly hoarse as he shouted.

Gillian turned to him, the blood draining from her face.

"What are you doing!?" she hissed, her voice still low.

"You said it might be one of the guys," said Nick defensively.

"Yeah, and it could be a fucking mountain lion for all we know!"

The rustling returned, closer and to the right.

Gillian hurriedly looked around her feet and quickly reached for something. Before Nick could ask, she stood with a large and sturdy stick clenched in both hands. As she gingerly stepped forward, Nick found himself stepping behind her.

"Chad? Marco?" called Gillian. "Is that you?"

Silence.

Gillian took another step forward. Nick placed a hand on her shoulder.

"Don't you think we should get help?" he said. "What if it *is* a lion?"

"Then we won't be able to outrun it," said Gillian, looking over her shoulder at him. She noticed Nick's terrified expression and smiled warmly. "Hey, if I get eaten, it gives you time to raise the alar-"

"Is someone there?" came a slight and feminine voice from the bushes.

Both counselors went rigid, their eyes widening. They stared in the direction of the voice.

"Hello?" called Gillian.

The rustling returned as a head slowly raised itself from behind a greatly overgrown and thorny bush. They could only see the top of the head and the person's eyes but the fear in them was apparent.

"Are you ok?" Gillian continued, taking a step forward.

The figure recoiled slightly, never taking her eyes off Gillian.

"Stick," the woman said.

Gillian looked at the stick in her hand.

"Sorry," she said. "We thought you might be a lion or something." Gillian passed the stick behind her. Nick took it and hid it between himself and Gillian. He was not ready to relinquish it just yet.

Gillian held up both her hands and took another step forward.

"The stick's gone, see? Are you ok? Are you hurt?"

"I saw him," said the stranger. "Is he here?"

"Is who here?"

"The shadow. He came and spoke to us. Did you see him?"

"We should go get help," whispered Nick.

"Give me a second," said Gillian replied, still staring at the stranger. "Why don't you come out?" she called. "Do you need food? Water? We don't have any on us, but we can get you some. Do you need a blanket? We can get you one of those too?"

The woman appeared hesitant. She nodded gingerly and came out from behind the bush. She was wearing a hospital gown that was filthy and damp. Her appearance shocked Gillian and elicited no small amount of sympathy: the stranger had obviously been out overnight, or at least appeared that way, and was in a state of considerable distress.

Around the woman's left wrist was a patient tag and her gown sported a familiar logo.

"Shit. She's from Lake Side," whispered Nick.

"What?" Gillian asked.

"Lake Side hospital. It's a mental asylum."

Gillian frowned.

"What the hell is she doing all the way out here?" she asked

"I don't like you two talking," said the woman. Her posture

had changed. She was ready to run.

"We're concerned, that's all," said Gillian. "It's not safe for you out here." She held out a welcoming hand and beckoned the stranger over. "Come with us. We have clothes and-"

The walkie talkie attached to her belt squawked with enough volume to make the three of them jump.

"Marco? Trixie?" came Stephen's voice.

The shock was enough. The stranger shrieked and ran, sprinting away from the counselors like her life depended on it. Before Gillian and Nick could react, she was in the woods and out of sight.

"Shit," cursed Gillian. "We need to go after her?"

"Us?" said Nick. "We need to call this in Gill! Get the police here."

Gillian did not hesitate. She grabbed the walkie talkie from her belt.

"Stephen? Chad? Anyone? We need help!"

*

Marco and Trixie heard the commotion via their own radio as they walked to the shower block. Something about a crazy lady running into the woods around the camp. Chad was taking charge and ordering Nick and Gillian to return to the main hut while he called the police.

Whatever it was, they did not care, and considering Marco's mood had yet to improve Trixie figured now was the best time for her ace in the hole.

Tapping him lightly on the shoulder, she reached into her back pocket and produced the crumpled but intact joint.

"Figured you needed cheering up," she said, smiling. Marco looked at the joint then to her and smiled too.

"You know me too well baby," he said, taking it from her with one hand while wrapping an arm around her waist. He pulled her close and began kissing her neck.

"Y'know, with everyone distracted, we've got some alone time," said Marco as he groped at Trixie. She knew him all too well and to refuse so soon after his foul mood could create a scene. HE did know how to turn her on, however, and she felt the familiar warmth spreading through her.

Why the hell not, she thought to herself. Taking his hand, she led him into the shower block.

★

The killer watched them necking passionately before they disappeared into the shower block. It would be so easy to kill them while they were distracted. He had the carving knife he had used to kill Wallace Asher hanging off his belt. He could walk in and stab them both, once each in the neck, and watch as their lives ended. It was a sight he found he quite enjoyed. It instilled him with power, the power of holding another person's life in his hands and extinguishing it through his own will.

And these kids, he would extinguish their lives with relish.

He had planned to commence the killings that night but seeing these two in the throes of teenage passion, oblivious to the world around them, made the killer impatient.

He clutched the handle of the carving knife with enough force to make his knuckles go white, pulled it from his waistband, and paced toward the shower block.

★

Lucy and Brandon had also heard the commotion on the radio. They had checked through most of the equipment in the shed and were just finishing the inventory of the archery gear when a follow up call came through from Chad asking all counselors to head back to the medical hut until the police arrived.

The two of them had no qualms. They downed tools and hurriedly left the shed.

Had they finished their inventory they would have noticed one of the bows, along with several arrows, were missing.

★

The shower block was filling with the haze of smoke and the herbal smell of weed as Trixie pushed her boyfriend hurriedly into the nearest cubicle and undid his belt. Sliding a hand down his pants, she smiled when she found him fully erect. He let out a long sigh of pleasure as he exhaled smoke. Passing the joint to Trixie, he slid his hand under her mini skirt, looped her underwear in his fingers and allowed them to drop to her ankles, where she stepped out of them.

They gazed at each other hungrily. Trixie smiled and blew smoke in her lover's face. As she suspected, his mood had improved considerably, and besides, he brought out a devious and sultry side of her she quite liked.

It was a shame he was terrible the rest of the time.

"Turn around," Marco ordered.

Trixie winked at him and did as she was told, standing on tip toes and lifting her skirt.

Marco could barely control himself. Releasing himself from his pants, he eagerly grabbed Trixie's hips and entered her.

★

The teens were energetic, there was no doubt about it. The killer stood outside the door to the block and listened with quiet amusement at the noises emanating from within. The girl moaned like an overly enthusiastic porn star while the boy grunted like a rutting gorilla.

The smell of cannabis was strong.

Easy prey, thought the killer as he brought the knife up and crossed the threshold into the shower block.

★

The radio in Elias's cruiser buzzed.

"Deputy Ansel? Come in."

Elias, who was stood by the open driver's side door and sipping his fifth coffee of the day, reached in and grabbed the radio.

"Ansel here," he said. "What's up Janet?"

"We got a call come in from Camp Summerside," said Janet. "Seems like they may have had a run in with one of your missing patients."

Ansel went white.

"Male or female?" he asked.

"Female. She ran off into the woods from the sounds of it. The counselors are safe but shaken."

"Thank you, Janet. I'm on my way."

Deputy Elias Ansel got into his cruiser and changed the radio frequency.

"Lieutenant Wiley, come in. It's Deputy Ansel."

The voice on the other end of the line sounded weary.

"What is it Ansel?" he asked.

"We have a potential sighting of Annette Maxwell down at Camp Summerside. I'm heading out there now but please send a cruiser to meet me. Sounds like there's a few frightened counselors that will need interviewing."

Wiley sighed. It was like Ansel could hear the man pinching the bridge of his nose.

"Will do, Deputy," he said and signed off.

Elias replaced the radio, put the car in drive, and headed away from Lake Side toward Camp Summerside at speed.

SUMMERSIDE LAKE MASSACRE

★

As Marco grunted in her ear, Trixie heard a noise she did not expect.

Footsteps.

They were approaching cautiously, though not quietly. Each footfall hit the wooden flooring with a dull thud.

"Marco," Trixie whispered.

Marco bit her shoulder and continued grinding, his focus entirely on his pleasure.

"Marco, *stop!* I hear something!" she hissed.

Her man ceased his gyrating with a disgruntled *huff* before hearing it himself.

Thud.

Marco quickly stepped away from Trixie and began to hurriedly pull up his pants. Trixie grabbed her underwear from the floor and stepped back into them, eyes wide with panic.

"Hey!" shouted Marco with more aggression than he actually felt.

The footsteps stopped outside their cubical.

The door rattled.

They wanted in.

"The fuck?" said Marco.

The door rattled again, in earnest this time. The sudden shaking caused Trixie to scream. Marco pushed himself back against the back wall, his face white.

"Hey man! That ain't funny!" he yelled.

The rattling stopped.

"Chad, if that's you you're a fuckin' dead man!" Marco shouted.

The door was hit with an almighty crash as the person's full body weight hit it at once. Trixie continued to scream as Marco, blind with panic, grabbed the top of the cubicle partition in a vain attempt to scramble over. As the attack against the cubicle door continued, he continued to shout threats.

Then, as quickly as it had started, the attack ended.

The sudden cessation of noise was practically deafening as Trixie and Marco stared apprehensively at the door.

"Hello?" said Marco, finding his voice.

The silence filled their ears for an agonisingly long time. Marco and Trixie looked at each other before she, finding a modicum of courage, began to reach for the lock.

"What's going on in there?" came a distant voice.

Outside the cubicle, the duo's assailant bolted, their footsteps thundering away toward the shower block's rear entrance where they disappeared.

"Jesus, what the hell is that smell?" came the voice again, louder this time, and suddenly familiar.

Trixie opened the lock and practically ran from the cubicle into the arms of Stephen Haig, where she wept.

TWENTY

When Sheriff Clark received the call from Deputy Elias Ansel he was sat in his cruiser already deeply engrossed in the research supplied to him by David Edwards at the *Summerside Gazette.*

Judge Atwell, it seemed, had been a bad man.

None of the paperwork stated sources other than a single alias named Waldo, who supplied the *Gazette* with enough evidence to permanently ruin the Judge's career and, if proven, eventually send him to prison.

While there were scandalous reports of him frequenting establishments for the purposes of soliciting sex, all outside Summerside Hills of course, it was the apparent embezzlement of government funding that could lead to a criminal conviction.

Doug had no idea who this Waldo was or how he came about this information, but it was clear they had a grudge against Atwell, one big enough to drive him to ruin the man for good.

"Sheriff, it's Ansel, you there?"

Doug sighed and grabbed the radio.

"Clark here," he said.

"You'd best get down to Camp Summerside chief," said Elias. "One of our escaped patients just made an appearance."

"Molyneux?"

"Annette Maxwell. I'm heading there now."

"I'm half an hour away," the Sheriff said, throwing the file with the rest of them on the passenger seat, turning on the ignition and driving away from the *Summerside Gazette*.

★

Young Officer Jackson amongst the chaos of the Heagney shooting. It did not sit right with him what had happened. The man was surrendering and unarmed, there was no reason to shoot him. The police had him surrounded; he would not have made it ten paces before being placed in handcuffs. Yet the simple motion of surrendering was enough for some trigger-happy asshole to unload their revolver, and once one gun goes off, a group of them do.

Wiley clearly did not give a shit.

He dared not report the Lieutenant though. While he had not seen it first-hand, Jackson was aware of his superior's reputation: a man with a temper, they said. One you did not want to fuck with. And Jackson could not raise the incident higher. Why would Wiley's bosses care? They would agree it was self-defence and put a line under it.

But the incident was still morally wrong. While he did not know why Heagney had been incarcerated, Jackson knew the difference between right and wrong within the eyes of the law, and gunning down an unarmed man was definitely wrong.

Wiley ordered him to stay at the crime scene to keep an eye on forensics, but Jackson knew he had been left there out of spite for the simple act of questioning the Lieutenant's authority. He had unwillingly made an enemy of the Lieutenant, but he would be damned if he would kiss ass to get back in his good books if it meant going against what he stood for.

Jackson excused himself and went for a walk away from the crime scene. He needed air..

Without noticing, he eventually found himself nearly half a mile away, his mind on auto-pilot dwelling on the events of the morning.

It was as he came to a moment of clarity and decided to return to his colleagues that a stranger casually walked from behind a tree, a queer smile on his face and his hands behind his back as if he were enjoying an early afternoon stroll.

"Hey there!" the man said cheerily, waving at Jackson. "Lovely day huh?"

The initial shock of seeing the stranger wore off quickly, and Jackson noticed the glaring and obvious problem: the stranger appeared ragged and dressed in tattered overalls.

It was the casual nature of the man's approach that had initially set Jackson at ease, but his deductive reasoning took over. With Heagney dead and Maxwell seen at Camp Summerside, that left only one person the stranger could be.

Jackson's face dropped and he quickly reached for his pistol. Unlike Heagney, he had no compunction gunning down Karl Molyneux.

Molyneux raised the pistol hidden behind his back and pointed it at the officer's head.

"Don't move," he said calmly. "Raise your hands slowly or I'll shoot you."

Jackson hesitated.

"If you fire that weapon, you'll have a whole swarm of officers here in no time," Jackson said.

"That's not strictly true," said Molyneux. "They're not *that* close. But I do need something from you and it's easier to get that if you're alive."

"What do you mean?"

"Take off your uniform," Karl said.

Jackson just stared.

"My uniform?" he asked.

"Did I stutter? Take off your uniform or I'll shoot you in the face."

Jackson frowned and shook his head.

"I'm not removing my uniform," he said defiantly.

"Suit yourself," said Karl. He squeezed the trigger, the bullet hitting Jackson between his nose and right eye. He was already dropping like a ragdoll as the exit wound sprayed his brains behind him and onto the forest floor.

Molyneux was on him immediately, unbuckling Jackson's belt and acutely aware of the commotion he had just caused.

★

The crack that reverberated through the woodland sounded much like a car backfiring but for the forensic team and two supervising officers the sound was all too familiar.

Officer Mills had been approaching Heagney's body when he heard it. Everyone looked in unison at the direction of the noise.

Mills pointed at one of the officers as he unholstered his weapon.

"You, come with me." He pointed at the second officer and said, "You, call it in."

Mills did not wait. He ran toward the gunshot with his pistol drawn.

★

Molyneux was quick. He was already hidden among the trees wearing the officer's ill-fitting uniform when Mills and his colleague arrived at the scene. He did not look back though he did smile when he heard the howls of rage from the them. He disappeared into the woods, now in full police uniform with two fully loaded pistols.

TWENTY-ONE

The scene at Camp Summerside was one of heightened emotions as Conrad Ellis rounded the corner to the entrance in his silver Mercedes Benz. He was concerned to find a police cruiser parked next to Stephen Haig's truck, and a Deputy questioning both Nick and Gillian.

He pulled the Benz to the other side of the truck. As he exited the vehicle, he could hear shouting coming from inside the medical hut. The voices sounded like Chad and Marco.

The Deputy saw Conrad and beckoned him over.

"Afternoon Deputy," said Conrad cheerily, though not without caution. "What's happened?"

"Conrad Ellis?" asked the Deputy.

"Yes."

The Deputy pointed toward the medical hut and said, "Can you calm your people down please while I finish my questioning? I'll need to speak to you when I'm done."

SUMMERSIDE LAKE MASSACRE

The yelling continued. Conrad nodded and approached the commotion.

In the hut he found Stephen, Chad, Marco, and Trixie. Marco and Chad were practically nose to nose as their respective tirades drowned each other out. Trixie was stood in the corner hugging herself, and appeared frightened. Stephen watched the young men wearily. He noticed Conrad and rolled his eyes.

To the left of the door was an air horn. This was usually used for activities but now seemed as good a time as any to use it. Conrad lifted it off the wall, held it over his head and pressed the button.

In the confines of the hut, the sound was deafening. Trixie covered her ears and screamed while Stephen closed his eyes. The two aggressors leapt back in shock and turned to the doorway.

Conrad placed the horn back in its pedestal.

"Right, now the pissing contest is done with, can someone kindly tell me what the hell is going on?"

"They fucked up, that's what's going on," said Chad.

"Fuck you," said Marco under his breath.

"One at a time please," Conrad demanded. "Chad?

"Yeah, let the pretty boy speak first, why don't you," said Marco.

"*Shut up!*"

The sudden outburst from Conrad shocked them all into silence. He stared at Marco with contempt. The two held eye contact for an uncomfortably long time before Marco relented.

He shifted in place and stared at his feet.

"You were saying Chad," Conrad said, not taking his eyes off Marco.

"Mr Haig caught them doing drugs in the shower block," he said.

"Stephen?" asked Conrad.

"It's true," said Haig. "You could smell it a mile off."

"Fucking peeping-tom is what he is," said Marco.

"What was that?" asked Conrad.

"What the hell was he doing hanging around the shower block anyway?" Marco protested. "You like creeping up on people do you?"

"If you had your radio on you would've known there was an incident that needed us all to meet back here," said Chad. "But you didn't have your radio on, did you? Stephen was looking for everyone for their own safety."

"Get fucked, *Chad*," Marco said with disdain. "If he was looking for our own safety, why'd he try and get into the cubicle with us huh?"

"What the hell you talkin' about?" asked Haig, offended.

"Now he plays dumb," sneered Marco. "Fucking pervert tried to get in with us. Practically broke the door down."

"Even *if* that were true," said Haig, "why would that make me a pervert? Unless you were doing somethin' else you shouldn't be?"

Marco turned bright red. Trixie shifted uncomfortably on her feet.

"Christ, really?" asked Chad. "In the shower block? You were meant to be cleaning it!"

Marco's mouth flapped as he tried to respond.

"Stephen, what's your side of story?" Conrad asked.

"I was on my way to see these two. Figured it'd be a good idea to check up on 'em, you know, make sure they weren't messin' around. By the time I got to the latrines the call came on the radio that there was a problem and seein' as the two of them weren't there I figured they'd be at the shower block. When I arrived, I could smell weed and could hear a commotion. When I shouted, askin' what's goin' on, Trixie ran out and practically fell on me. I thought Marco had been nasty to her or somethin', but they kept babblin' on about some creep tryin' to get in."

"Convenient you showed up when you did huh?" said Marco sarcastically.

"I'm going to say this now," said Conrad to Marco, "if there is another word from you in the next five minutes, I'll throw you in the lake. Clear?"

Marco scoffed.

"Yeah? Try it."

"I've got one better for you. How about I tell the officer out there you've been dealing in illegal substances? Maybe tell them to search the shower block. I'm sure they'd find something interesting that will support my story. Something casually discarded?"

Marco went silent. Conrad looked over at Trixie.

"Is there anything you'd like to add?" he asked.

Trixie sheepishly looked between the men in the room. Conrad could not help but feel sorry for her. She was a good kid. Why the hell was she going with someone like Marco? It might be worth keeping them separate for the time being.

She shook her head.

"Either of you made a statement to the officer outside?" asked Conrad.

They both shook their heads.

"Right, both of you get out and speak to him. The grown-ups need to talk."

★

The Sheriff arrived as two grumpy looking teenagers exited the medical hut and walked toward Deputy Ansel. They did not speak to one another, but as the boy attempted to place an arm around the girl, she shrugged him off and stepped away. The look on the boy's face was cold and angry.

Doug parked behind Elias's cruiser and exited his vehicle. The Deputy and the Sheriff acknowledged each other. As Elias continued to talk to two other teenagers - a bone white young girl with enormous, vibrant red hair and a skinny black kid in shorts with large thick rimmed glasses - the Deputy pointed his pen at the medical hut.

Doug walked towards the hut to find Conrad Ellis.

★

SUMMERSIDE LAKE MASSACRE

Lucy and Brandon approached the central green to see the commotion. They both recognised the Sheriff as he stood from his car and could see Gillian and Nick being questioned. Trixie and Marco were approaching the Deputy but stood away from each other.

"Lover's tiff?" asked Lucy playfully.

"Bit more than that, I'd say. Marco looks like he wants to kill someone."

"He *always* has that face," Lucy said as she yawned. "It all looks very serious."

Brandon looked at his girlfriend curiously. She had heard the message on the radio, same as him, and judging by the panic in the voices of both Nick and Gillian, along with the arrival of the Sheriff, there was something very serious happening. But Lucy did not appear bothered at all.

"We should probably go meet them," he said, unsure of what else to say. "The police will likely want to speak to us."

"To us?" Lucy laughed, nervously. "Why us? We didn't do anything."

"I know that, but they have to ask us where we were, what we were doing, who were we with, you know?" He leaned in conspiratorially. "Make sure you're not an escaped mental patient."

"They can't possibly think it's me?" she asked.

"Well, of course not dummy. But they have to question everyone don't they?"

Lucy frowned. Brandon rolled his eyes and took her hand.

He could never tell what she was thinking.

"C'mon," he said and walked toward the Deputy.

★

"We fire them, pure and simple," said Chad. "They're a liability." Conrad made to speak but Chad held up a hand to stop him. "I know what you're going to say, and no, I don't like Marco, never have, but we've had a legitimate emergency today and the two of them are off getting high and getting laid. We can't rely on them."

Conrad nodded. "Fair enough. What about you Stephen?" He asked the caretaker.

"I think Trixie should get a second chance," he said. "I think she's a decent kid at heart, she just got with the wrong guy. But Marco needs to go. Chad's right, we can't rely on him. What if someone got hurt today? What if a kid gets hurt while he's meant to be watchin' 'em? We can't have someone like that around and with him gone, I guarantee Trixie will improve."

Conrad nodded and motioned the two of them to the office. They followed as their boss sat at the desk. Stephen opened the bottom drawer, and pulled out the bottle of scotch.

"Go grab three glasses for us would you kid?" he said to Chad.

Chad looked from his boss to the liquor and smiled.

"But I'm underage," he said. "And there're cops outside."

"So, you'd better hurry then," said Conrad.

SUMMERSIDE LAKE MASSACRE

Chad turned and exited the office eagerly. Conrad waited until he was out of sight before turning to the caretaker.

"Do you know anyone that can replace Marco with this kind of notice?" he asked.

Stephen shook his head.

"I don't I'm afraid," he replied.

Conrad nodded.

"Me neither, and therein lies the problem," said Conrad as he stood and looked out the office window. The view was unremarkable, with patches of long grass leading up to an overgrown part of the surrounding woods. "No one else applied. Finding a replacement before camp opens won't be possible. You know as well as I that we can't open with fewer counselors than we already have. It's a safety issue. It won't look good."

"Can I speak freely?" asked Stephen.

"This isn't the military," said Conrad with a smile. "You can say what you like. You disagree?"

"In part, yes," said the caretaker. "I don't doubt that findin' a replacement mid-season will be possible. Plenty of other kids in town, and there's bound to be one of 'em willing to step in. It's keepin' Marco on until then I disagree with. If there's anythin' that's come out this afternoon, it's how self-centred he is. He *knows* he messed up and he had every opportunity to apologise, but he didn't. He's the kind of kid that would throw an old lady under a bus and blame the driver for not missin' her."

"That's a pretty strong judgement," said Conrad.

Haig shrugged.

"I've seen plenty characters like that in my time," he said. "It'll take juvie to straighten him out, and even then, that ain't a guarantee."

Conrad sighed and sat back down at his desk.

"I don't disagree with you on his character Stephen, but the fact is that when our guests arrive, we need a full team. Hell, I'd even argue six isn't enough but that's the number Wallace gave me, so he get's the benefit of the doubt. We can't afford to lose him, not just yet. Besides, kids like him are cowards at heart. You just need to bring the fear of god down on them."

"So, he's stayin'," said Stephen, annoyed.

"He's staying," replied Conrad.

"And how do you intend to keep him in line?"

"I'll tell him I kept a little something from his time in the shower block that could find its way to the police."

"Chad ain't gonna be happy."

"Why do you think I sent him on his errand?" said Conrad, smiling. "Let me deal with Chad. And if he doesn't see reason, that's too bad I'm afraid."

The knock at the door distracted them. Both men turned to see the Sheriff stood in the doorway.

"Afternoon gentlemen," he said, nodding toward Conrad. "Mr Ellis, I presume?"

"You presume correctly."

"Sheriff Douglas Clark," said Doug, stepping forward and holding out his hand. Conrad shook it. "Can I talk to you for a moment? In private?"

Conrad glanced at Stephen.

"Would you give us a moment please?" he asked.

The caretaker nodded and walked past the Sheriff and out the hut.

★

After the Deputy had finished his questions, both Gillian and Nick had wondered to the nearest bench where they had sat in silence. The events of the afternoon were peculiar, though Gillian kept coming back to the woman and the fear in her eyes.

The Deputy had moved on to questioning Trixie while Marco stood to one side, his arms crossed, his face like thunder. Lucy and Brandon were also waiting their turn, though stood away from Marco. It seemed best to keep clear.

Gillian spotted Chad walking toward the medical hut with three glasses in his hand, where he was met by Mr Haig, who said something to him that caused some annoyance. Stephen put a hand on Chad's shoulder and walked him back the way he had come.

"You ok?" asked Nick.

"Yeah, just confused, that's all," she replied.

"Confused?" asked Nick.

"What was she doing out there? She must have been out overnight. Did you see? Her gown was soaked. Poor woman."

"Weren't you scared?"

Gillian shook her head and said, "I can't say I was. Strange, isn't it?"

Nick looked aghast.

"You weren't afraid at all?" he asked. "I was shitting my pants."

Gillian nodded and laughed.

"Yes, I did notice that," she said.

"Hey!"

"Oh, don't be so offended you goofball," she said, nudging him with her elbow. "It *was* scary, I guess."

"But you weren't afraid," said Nick.

"I don't think so, no." Gillian turned to him with a smirk. "I guess I'm not normal then."

Nick was unsure how to respond. He sighed and watched Trixie sob as the Deputy turned his attention to Marco. Trixie wiped her nose, saw the two of them staring at her, and began to walk over.

"Look alive," Gillian said quietly to Nick.

Trixie surprised them both by smiling and pointing to the open spot on the bench.

"Got room for one more?" she asked.

"Oh, sure," said Gillian as she moved over. Trixie sat down, crossed her legs, and ran her hands through her hair.

"I want to go home," she said.

"I second that," said Nick. He looked at her. She was shaken, though, unless she had also met their escaped patient, he could not understand why.

"You ok?" he asked.

Trixie sighed and shook her head.

"No," she said honestly.

"What happened?" Nick asked.

"Hey, maybe now's not the best time to be asking that," Gillian interrupted. She turned toward Trixie. "But you'll be ok, right?"

Tears began to well up and as she wiped them away, she offered a quick nod. Gillian put an arm around her and pulled her close.

"Besides, we're safe now," said Gillian. "The police are here. We're safe now."

None of them had any way of knowing that one of them, despite their best efforts, would be dead before the day was out.

TWENTY-TWO

"What can I do for you Sheriff?" asked Conrad as Doug took the seat opposite him.

"I've been informed there's been an incident here this afternoon. Is that correct?" asked Doug.

Conrad appeared confused for a moment.

"You know," he said, "I haven't had the chance to speak to your Deputy. I just got back from a meeting in town and your man started ordering me around."

Doug raised an eyebrow. "You don't know?" he asked

Conrad shrugged.

"There was a situation at Lake Side hospital last night," said the Sheriff. "It's the mental institution for the state. A number of the inmates were able to escape."

"My god," said Conrad, his eyes widening.

"Three of them unaccounted for this morning. One has been caught, but there are still two we haven't found yet. It would appear as though your counselors may have had a run in with one of them."

Conrad slumped in his chair.

"I don't know what to say," he said.

"They were lucky not to have been hurt," said Clark.

Conrad nodded and said, "What does this mean for opening the Camp?"

"I'd strongly advise you either postpone the opening day until our missing patients are found or cancel altogether."

"Cancel?"

Doug nodded.

"That's quite out of the question I'm afraid," said Conrad. "We need the money from this year's season to fund next years. Cancelling would be catastrophic."

"I'm not sure you're quite aware of just how dangerous a situation this is," said the Sheriff, firmly. "One of the missing inmates is a man by the name of Karl Molyneux. Are you aware who that man is?"

Conrad nodded.

"Then I'm guessing you're aware that he murdered eight people back in '59, one of them a young girl. During his escape last night, he killed two of my Deputies."

Conrad looked solemn.

"I'm sorry to hear that Sheriff," he said.

"I appreciate it, but that doesn't change things. Molyneux is thought to be armed and is a danger to everyone while he's loose."

"And what's currently happening in order to catch this man?"

"We are liaising with state police, who have roadblocks in place at regular intervals. We are also utilising our resources to help facilitate search parties around the county."

"So, it's in hand then?" asked Conrad.

The Sheriff stared.

"Excuse me?" he said.

Conrad said, "I'll be straight with you; we cannot cancel this year's season. Postpone it, maybe, but even that will likely result in significant monetary loss. Now, I'm not suggesting at all that the lives of your Deputies are worth less than the monetary value of this camp. Their loss is a genuine tragedy. I am, however, a businessman and in order for this Camp to continue, we *need* this season to happen. I'm not just thinking about myself here either. There's a knock-on effect too. Parents send their children here for all kinds of reasons: work commitments, vacations, some good old-fashioned peace and quiet, and so on. If we postpone, let alone close, then the whole town will suffer. As I'm sure you know, money from the camp goes into a whole bunch of initiatives within Summerside Hills. If Camp closes, they don't receive their funding. So, while I appreciate your concern, you must understand that it isn't as simple as just closing, especially with less than two days before we open."

The Sheriff considered this. Mr Ellis was correct, of course, but that did not mean he had to like it. For Doug, the safety of those at the camp greatly outweighed any monetary loss. But it was not just Conrad he had to convince. Like the man said, there would be a lot of disappointed children, angry parents, and disgruntled volunteers. All of that would be forgotten, however, if it came to light that the season went ahead while Karl Molyneux was still loose.

"You say you have roadblocks in place, correct?" asked Conrad.

"That is correct," Doug replied.

"And you're implying that every law enforcement officer in the state is involved in the man's apprehension?" Ellis continued.

"We are one-hundred percent dedicated to ensuring Karl Molyneux is caught or killed."

"Then, I have to say Sheriff, I have every faith that you will find him before we open," Conrad said, smiling. "I'm not being trivial here. It sounds like you're doing everything in your power to keep the town safe."

The Sheriff stood and nodded.

"Thank you for your time, Mr Ellis," he said. "I regret to say that I will be returning in the next twenty-four hours with a written order from Judge Atwell that Camp Summerside is to be closed until further notice. If you refute the order, you will have to face the Judge and present just cause."

Conrad frowned.

"Come on Sheriff, there's no need for that."

"I'm afraid there is. Am I clear?" asked Doug.

"Yes Sheriff, perfectly clear, but just so we're on the same page, until that order comes, I will continue to work towards

Camp Summerside opening the day after next. I must also say that I will find it incredibly disappointing if your department and state police can't apprehend a very dangerous criminal with the number of resources you have. I might find myself very vocal about that fact."

"I'm sure you will," said the Sheriff, "and you wouldn't be the first. In the interim, I advise you and the counselors leave and stay home. It will be announced within the hour that a county wide curfew will be put in effect until Molyneux is found. Should the curfew still be in place by the time you plan to open for the season, you will find yourself in violation of that curfew. Just a heads up."

"I appreciate the warning."

Douglas Clark went to leave but stopped and turned back to face Conrad.

"Please heed the danger Mr Ellis," he said. "If not for you, then for your staff."

Doug turned and walked from the building.

Conrad waited until the Sheriff was gone before he took the bottle of scotch, removed the cork, and drew an almighty swig. As he turned to look out the rear office window, he placed the cork back in the bottle and sighed.

*

Deputy Elias Ansel walked to his cruiser. He was angry.

He had interviewed the counselors and it seemed no-one had

been harmed, physically at least. Annette Maxwell could be anywhere by now and Ansel was growing impatient at the lack of back-up from Wiley.

As he grabbed his radio, he saw the Sheriff exit the medical hut also looking thoroughly annoyed.

"Lieutenant Wiley, this is Deputy Elias Ansel, come in."

Sheriff Clark approached and waited with him for the reply.

"Lieutenant Wiley, please come in. This is Deputy Ansel."

The was a brief flurry of static before an agitated voice said, "What is it Deputy?"

"Lieutenant Wiley, we're in real need of back up here at Camp Summerside to look for one of our escaped patients. Where are the Officers that were promised?"

"I've got bigger problems than you right now, Ansel. Molyneux just shot one of my new recruits point blank in the face and took his service weapon and his uniform. Frankly, I couldn't give a fuck about Camp Summerside right now."

Doug took the radio from Elias as the Deputy stared at it in disbelief.

"Wiley, this is Sheriff Clark. When did this happen?"

"What does it matter?"

"It matters on how much of a head start he has."

There was a sigh on the other end of the radio.

"A half hour ago, give or take," said Wiley.

"Did the APB I requested earlier get put out?"

"You think I'm stupid?" asked Wiley. "His face is out to every cop in the state. I know what I'm doing Clark."

The Sheriff checked his watch. It had just gone five. Still another hour till the evening papers would be released.

And the roads are manned, he thought. *What else could they do?*

"Roger Lieutenant," said Doug. "And I'm sorry about your man. Truly."

There was another sigh.

"Appreciate it Sheriff," said Wiley. "Anything else?"

"That's all for now."

The radio went silent.

"That's it?" asked Elias.

"What else *can* we do?" asked the Sheriff. "We have all our guys and all of Wiley's out looking for our suspect, the roadblocks are in place, every cop in the state has his photograph, and we'll have the curfew in place this evening. Short of calling in the national guard, I can't think of much more we can throw at this."

"What about Maxwell?"

"Did you see her rap sheet?"

Elias nodded and said, "She has severe manic depression brought on by extreme post-traumatic stress, though her file didn't say what the cause was."

"Is she dangerous?"

"To herself, sure, though she's never shown signs of aggression to anyone else. Fear, certainly, but never violence."

"Double check her description was included in the APB, but Molyneux remains the focus. We'll ask the public to be vigilant for them both, but I don't see Maxwell being as significant a threat."

"There's a first time for everything boss," said Elias.

"Dammit, I know that!" Doug snapped. "I'm not leaving her out to dry! But we also need to prioritise. I mean, Jesus, Molyneux's killed three police officers in less than twenty-four hours! We *must* catch him."

Elias stared at his boss. There was no time he could remember ever seeing the Sheriff so worked up. The psychopath's evasion of both the police and the county Sheriff's office was beginning to eat away at his boss. The Sheriff was correct of course. Annette Maxwell was an unknown quantity, but Karl Molyneux absolutely needed to be caught and quickly.

Elias nodded. "What do you intend to do now?" he asked.

"Head back to the office," said Doug. "At least then, if anything comes up, people will know where to find me. Why don't you go home, huh? It's been a long day for both of us."

"I can sleep later. Right now, I want to drive around where Molyneux was last seen. It's a long shot but you never know. I might find something."

"Be careful," the Sheriff said.

Elias smiled.

"I will."

TWENTY-THREE

onrad exited the administrative hut as both the Sheriff and his Deputy left the camp grounds. He watched them go with contempt. He was not a man that liked to be threatened but for appearances sake he was willing to give the Sheriff some leeway.

The counselors were all staring at him. Even the caretaker appeared to be looking to him for guidance.

I'm the boss, he thought, realising he was starting to resent the responsibility this currently entailed.

"Can you all gather round please," he said. His staff all stood and headed toward him.

"What did the Sheriff want?" called Chad as he approached.

"Can we go home?" Trixie asked.

"You'll have all noticed that we've had an incident here this afternoon," said Conrad, looking between the group as they all stared at him urgently. "Fortunately, no one was hurt but I think it's safe to say we're all a little shaken, agreed?"

They all nodded, except Marco, who appeared disinterested as he stared toward the trees.

"I've spoken with the Sheriff, and I feel it's prudent to inform you what he told me. There was an incident last night at the Lake Side hospital. I'm assuming you all know where Lake Side is?"

They nodded again.

"It would seem there was a technical malfunction that resulted in a couple of the inmates leaving their cells. Everything's fine, the police have handled it, but there are still two patients that are unaccounted for. One of them was the lady Gillian and Nick saw today."

"What does that mean for us?" asked Nick.

"What do you mean?" Conrad said.

"I mean for us now, for the camp opening, for the town, for everything."

"Glad you asked," said Conrad as he slid his hands into his pockets. "The Sheriff has advised that we postpone the opening of the camp until the missing patients have been found." There was muted nodding among the group. "He has, however, advised that every cop in the county is currently involved in the search. He also advised that the patients are not explicitly dangerous, but they are ill, and therefore unpredictable, which is why he has advised delaying the opening day. Now, before any of you ask anything, I would like to say my piece.

"Obviously, delaying the opening of camp will be a pain for

everyone, including our campers. I am, however, entirely confident the police will be able to do their job, which will mean opening the camp, as intended, two days from now. As such, I am yet to make a full decision on what option to take going forward."

Gillian raised his hand.

"Yes?" asked Conrad.

"Are you suggesting we carry on as normal, after Trixie told me they were attack in the shower block by a madman?"

"What!?" shouted Lucy. "I thought we were talking about a crazy lady in the woods!"

"Did you see who it was?" asked Brandon, concerned.

"Wait a minute, calm down!" Conrad voice echoed across the group. "We don't need any more fuel to the fire!"

"So, what are you suggesting?" said Chad.

"I'm suggesting we need time to think. All of us, as a group. And it's been a hell of an afternoon for you all, I can tell, so I don't think it's suitable to make any decisions on this right now."

"I just want to go home," said Trixie. "Please?"

"I could use a beer," Stephen said.

"I second that," laughed Chad.

"I'm with Trixie on this," said Gillian. "I'd prefer to go home if it's all the same with you guys."

Conrad nodded.

"We don't need to make the decision now," he said. "Let's regroup here bright and early tomorrow and discuss this fully." He stared at his watch and yawned. "I won't lie, I'd quite like a drink too now it's been mentioned," he said. "Buddy's in town will be open wont it Steve?"

Stephen nodded.

"Well," Conrad said, "it'll be a squeeze but there's enough room between my car and Stephen's truck to be this evening's ride home. Who wants some food? My dollar."

Trixie hugged herself and shook her head.

Conrad sighed. "Who wants to go home?" he asked.

Trixie and Gillian raised their hands, followed by Nick. Brandon raised his and frowned when Lucy did not follow suit.

"Marco?" asked Conrad.

"Just drop me in town," he said, looking off into the trees.

"I thought you were staying at mine tonight?" Brandon quietly asked Lucy.

"Well, I still can, but why not get some free food first, huh?" she said playfully.

Brandon continued to frown.

"But my parents are out tonight?" he continued. "I was going to cook us something nice, make an evening of it."

She turned and smiled, placing a hand on his cheek.

"Oh Brandon," she said. "That is sweet of you, but that can wait can't it?" She turned her gaze toward Conrad as Brandon seethed at her condescending tone.

"Ok, so it's settled then," Conrad beamed. "Those going home, come with me. The rest of you, head to Buddy's with Mr Haig, and I'll meet you there."

The group walked towards the waiting vehicles. Lucy took

Brandon's hand and walked a couple of paces before she met resistance. She turned to her boyfriend, confused, when she saw his clenched jaw.

"C'mon," she said. "We're going to Buddy's"

"No, I'm not," said Brandon.

"What do you mean? I thought we'd just agreed?" Lucy said, confused.

"When?"

"When what?"

"When did we agree we'd go to Buddy's?"

The expectant, haughty look on her face made his blood boil. Back in the early days of their relationship Brandon thought that look was sweet, a sign she cared. Now, it was belittling to the point of insulting.

"Just now you big goof," giggled Lucy, giving his arm another tug. Brandon did not budge.

"Really?" he said, his anger boiling. "Just now? We had a conversation just this second where I categorically told you I'd like to join you and the others for dinner?"

Lucy's confusion continued as she said, "Well, not like that, but-"

"We had a conversation where I told you that?" Brandon interrupted. "Where, despite me having spent a bunch of money on getting the things I need to treat you to a nice romantic evening, an evening that you *knew* I was planning, despite *all* of that, I'm going to abandon those plans at the drop of a hat because *you* suddenly want to do something else? We had that conversation, did we? Because all I got was you changing your mind and expecting *me* to follow. Like you *always* do!"

The others, having moved toward the stationary vehicles, turned as Brandon's voice raised in volume and hostility. Lucy's perplexed expression had morphed into stunned silence. Her boyfriend had never spoken to her with such anger before tonight and, until that very second, she had never thought he was capable of it. She had not thought of their plans, or her sudden change in mind, or even that doing so would aggravate him in such a way. It did not even occur to her that such a decision on her part would be the final straw in a series of incidents that she had dismissed immediately yet he had dwelled on. At that moment, all she could think was that she had just been yelled at by her boyfriend, in front of a crowd.

The embarrassment was overwhelming.

Behind her, she heard Stephen's truck coughing and failing to start but it was distant, as if underwater.

"I'm...sorry," she said, unsure what else to say.

Brandon stared at his girlfriend a moment longer before snatching his hand from hers and looking at the group, whose attention was turned toward the vehicles. Their expressions were worried.

"What's the problem?" he called, brushing past Lucy as we walked toward them.

"They're dead," said Chad.

"What are?" Brandon asked as he noticed the hood of Stephen's truck was up with the caretaker huddled over the engine. Stephen cursed under his breath as Conrad opened the hood of his own car.

"The spark plug's gone," said the caretaker. "Conrad?"

Conrad's own curse came as he stood up from the engine and dropped the hood.

"Gone," he said.

"Gone, what does that mean?" asked Trixie.

"It means that the cars aren't going anywhere," Conrad said.

"What?" she said, panicked.

"Hey, it's cool," said Chad to Trixie. "We'll just use the radio, get a tow truck and a taxi and we can get out of here." He smiled at her. She smiled back. Marco noticed.

As Chad jogged toward the medical hut, Stephen shut the hood of his truck and wiped his hands on his pants.

"So, who did it?" he asked.

"Did…what?" asked Nick.

"Who took the spark plugs?" asked the caretaker. "C'mon, they don't just up and walk, so someone must've taken 'em. Whoever's got 'em hand 'em over."

"Conrad!" Chad cried with enough fear for the group to run toward the office. Conrad and Stephen were through the door first as the others pushed their way in. They found Chad in the office, pale, and stood opposite the radio. The radio itself was smoking, its front panel pulled off and its internal circuits fried. It was dripping wet and as the men peered to the floor, the smell in the room told them the culprit was the bottle of scotch. The bottle lay empty on the floor.

SUMMERSIDE LAKE MASSACRE

The line to the wall mounted phone had also been cut. The receiver was snapped in two and hanging uselessly.

"What the hell Chad!?" shouted Stephen.

"Hey, it wasn't me man!" said the counselor in defence. "I called as soon as I saw it!"

"What's happening?" asked Nick from outside the office as they heard footsteps approaching behind them. Those outside turned to see Brandon running at them in a state of distress. No one had noticed his absence and they were disquieted to see the harried, stricken look on his face.

"What's wrong?" asked Gillian as her colleague came to a stop.

"I can't find her," Brandon said, out of breath.

"Can't find who?" asked Conrad as he stepped from the office, Stephen still glaring at Chad, and stood in the entrance to the hut.

"Lucy, I can't find her!" said Brandon.

"What do you mean you can't find her?" asked Trixie.

"I mean, *I can't find her!*" Brandon nearly screamed before staring at Conrad desperately. "She's gone!"

PART THREE

THE MASSACRE

"What do you want!?"
"To see what your insides look like."
Scream, 1996

TWENTY-FOUR

"**S**he can't have just vanished," said Marco, whose tough veneer was eroding as panic spread among the group. "I mean, she's not a fucking kid, man. She's probably off pouting or something."

"Where did you last see her?" Conrad asked Brandon.

"Over there, in the middle of the green," said Brandon, pointing to where they had been standing. "I just assumed she would walk over to the cars. That's where we all were."

"Did she have any reason to wonder off?" said Conrad.

Brandon appeared sheepish.

"Well, I was hard on her," he said. "When you guys heard me shouting? I was pissed. There's been times she's bugged me and it all came to a head." He hung his head. "I shouldn't have shouted at her."

Conrad placed a consoling hand on the boy's shoulder and said, "What's done is done. She couldn't have gone far. The site isn't *that* big. Like Marco said, she probably went for a walk to clear her head."

"Not to put too fine a point on it," said Stephen, "but we have bigger things to worry about. The spark plugs from both our vehicles have vanished and the radio has been destroyed."

"The radio's *destroyed!?*" Trixie cried.

Stephen nodded and said, "Yes, along with the phone. It looks deliberate. Also, spark plugs don't just disappear either so, that means someone here is responsible for both."

He turned to Chad, who was stood in the hut's doorway.

"You," he scalded.

"Me?" asked Chad.

"Yes, you. Care to explain yourself?" Stephen said as he folded his arms across his chest.

"Hey, don't pin this on me!" Chad said, incredulously. "I told you, I called as soon as I saw it!"

"You expect me to believe that?"

"It's the truth! When would I have had time to do it, huh?" Chad asked. "In the thirty seconds it took for me to walk from the truck to the office? Bullshit! You may as well accuse Conrad; he was in there before me!"

"Hey, hey," said Conrad. "Let's all calm down, shall we?"

"Tell him to back off then!" shouted Chad.

"C'mon Stephen," Conrad said. "You don't really think he did it, do you? And he's right, I was in there before him so you can just as easily point the finger at me."

"So, you did it," said Marco, smugly.

"Yes Marco, I, the camp owner, destroyed our only way to communicate with the outside world and ensure the only vehicles at our disposal are rendered completely useless. Now, do you have anything constructive to add, or are you going to shut up and let the adults talk?"

Marco's face bloomed red with rage.

"Say that again!" he said as he stepped toward Conrad. His boss turned to face him and braced himself for confrontation before Stephen stepped between them and placed a hand on Marco's chest.

"None of that now, son," he said as the counselor pushed against him.

"Get your hands off me!"

"Or what? I'm a dead man?" said Stephen. "You gonna take on everyone here, or you gonna help?"

Marco stared at the caretaker and held his gaze until his jaw relaxed and his clenched fists softened.

He exhaled and said, "Sorry, you're right. This isn't helping." He turned away briefly before the rage returned, his right hand balled into a fist, and he swung at Stephen. The caretaker, expecting this, took a step back and watched the fist fly past his face. The miss sent Marco off balance, and he stumbled to his left before falling forward. His momentum kept him turning, and as he fell he hit the ground on his right side with an *oomph*. The other counselors watched in amusement, barely containing their sniggers.

Stephen walked over as Marco rolled onto his back. The

caretaker held out a hand.

"C'mon, get up."

Marco smacked the hand away.

"Get the fuck away from me," he said as he scurried onto his feet. He dusted himself off and stared among the group. "You fucking people! Think you're better than me, is that it? Get a good fucking look, then, c'mon! Look at this fucking face and remember it, because I'm fucking out of here!"

He pivoted on his heels and stormed toward the entrance to the camp. The group said nothing as they just watched him go.

As he passed under the CAMP SUMMERSIDE arch, Nick said, "Shouldn't one of us stop him?"

"Why?" asked Chad.

"We're miles away from anywhere and it'll be dark soon, that's why."

"Leave him," said Stephen. "Either he'll come to his senses, or he'll walk the ten miles to town. Either way, he made his choice."

"He'll come back," said Trixie. "He always does, and he'll be just as mad."

"He can wait," said Conrad. "We've got bigger things to worry about than him. First, we find Lucy. Then we need to find out what the hell is happening around here because if none of you are responsible for the cars or the radio, which I haven't ruled out by the way, then we have to ask who is?"

★

SUMMERSIDE LAKE MASSACRE

Annette Maxwell, having fled Camp Summerside some hours earlier in a state of panic, continued to run into the woods, her mind a furnace of extreme anxiety, until she stopped and concluded she was well and truly lost. She was both cold and thirsty, and in no position to rectify either issue as the sun went down on the second night of her freedom.

Yet she did not feel free. She had not known freedom for quite some time.

Her respite from captivity would be short lived, this she knew, for once she was found she would be taken back to her cell at the hospital and medicated within an inch of her life. She was forced to take these meds every evening despite her pleas, yet she understood that a doped patient was far more compliant than one with their faculties intact.

Though, when you are one of many in a building built for housing the insane, trying to convince the powers that be you are of sound mind was impossible. She had come close to losing it many times, yet the less she was believed the more hopeless she became.

Her will had deteriorated to numbness.

Then the man in black arrived.

He was stood outside her cell door when he spoke. She did not think him real at first. She had taken her evening medication and was far from cognisant, yet the more he spoke, the more she rallied to that voice.

From his hooded shroud he appeared as if Death himself had become manifest, yet his voice was soft and reassuring. He told her she would be free and soon. He had put a plan in motion to rid her of her shackles. She did not speak, just listened, and when he told her to wait for her release, she did not question him.

It was less than an hour later when the maglocks to her cell clicked, and the door slid open. She did not think, she just ran. As the other inmates meandered around in confusion, many scared by the storm outside, others refusing to leave their cells, she bolted for the exit and freedom.

The man in black had promised and delivered. But escaping was only part of it. She had to remain free.

Stumbling across the teens at Camp Summerside had been accidental. Annette had no idea where she was heading and after seeing the two police officers ruthlessly gunned down, she had sprinted in any direction her feet chose. She eventually stopped running and, soaked through and deeply cold, found a disused hunting hideaway where she rested as the sun came up. It was only two hours later, after sleeping so deeply that not even a passing freight train could wake her, she woke, thoroughly disorientated, dehydrated, and still high from her medication. She would need to find help and soon.

As she climbed from the hideaway Annette heard the lapping of nearby water and, having seen the crystal blue waters of the lake from her room, eagerly strolled in the direction of the potential water source.

As the trees began to thin, Annette became aware of two large log cabins that were vaguely familiar. Their presence was concerning, as structures would mean people, however their familiarity sparked in her a fear that hit her like a tidal wave. Her memory, though, was patchy at best, not least due to the cocktail of drugs that filled her veins during the years of her internment, and the further back in time she tried to remember the less she could recall.

How many years had she been a patient? Annette was a young lady when she first arrived and now, whenever she looked in the mirror, she saw a haggard version of the beauty she used to be.

So, what was it from that forgotten past that was triggering her now? Something made her stomach drop, her chest tighten, and her mind to race.

She then saw the teenagers and the fear amplified. It had been so long since she had seen anyone other than doctors and orderlies. They were maybe seventeen or eighteen years old, graduate year or nearing it. One was a skinny black kid wearing battered glasses, a blue Summerside Hills High-School t-shirt, and camouflage shorts, and the other was a short, freckled ginger girl, with enormous, bristly hair and bone China skin. Her clothes were extraordinarily baggy; an oversized t-shirt and thick bell-bottomed jeans which was odd considering the heat of the day. They were a strange pairing to be sure, but Annette could see by their body language that they were comfortable in each other's company.

Annette stepped on a dead branch. The crack that emanated may as well have been a cannon firing.

Now, a few hours later, the sun setting, and totally lost, Annette wished she had stayed with the kids. The ginger girl seemed friendly though her black friend was clearly scared. Annette was unsurprised considering how she must have looked, but her general distrust of people had got the better of her so she ran. In hindsight they could have helped her. Sure, she would likely be back in her cell, but she would at least be warm, dry, and fed. If she continued to be free her options were limited, not least because she was an escaped mental patient.

But while the Asylum would be familiar, Annette absolutely knew that being there was never her choice to begin with.

She started to notice just how dark the woods around her were, and with no source of light on her, she would struggle making any further progress. She did not, however, relish another night in the woods.

She finally took stock of where she was and listened. Among the ambience of the wind through the trees and the birds singing in their nests, she was certain she heard the distant sound of a car drive by. It was faint but there, carried on the wind like signal. She remained still until she heard another one. The road could not have been far. While passing cars may mean capture, it may also mean shelter, food, and warmth. Remaining still would mean death.

Annette stumbled in the direction of the road and hoped that the light of dusk would be enough to illuminate her way.

★

Dean Elton had been the proprietor of the Hill Side motel,

situated five miles from the town, for fifteen years and thought he had seen everything.

The motel itself was shy of thirty-five years old, had twenty rooms in total, and had been the scene of many instances of ugliness over its lifetime.

Room Twenty was the particular favourite of an unpleasant man that simply called himself Chuck. Chuck would arrive on the first day of every month and rent room twenty. He frequented so regularly that he stopped asking Dean if the room was available, he simply showed up and was presented the key. Chuck would hand over an envelope that contained the cost of the room, thirty dollars for one night, as well as another two hundred for Dean's silence. Chuck always brought with him an old suitcase that Dean assumed contained some unsavoury items. During his stay, Chuck was visited by a woman who would bring her own suitcase and stay the night. By the time Chuck left the following day, his suitcase was noticeably lighter, and his female companions' was significantly heavier. They would shake hands and drive away separately, Chuck away from town, and his companion toward it.

But less than a year ago Dean had his first no show from Chuck. Two weeks later there was a story in the *Summerside Gazette* about a local drug gang taken down by the state police. Dean had sweated days afterward, certain the Sheriff or even the FBI would come calling, but they never did.

Goodbye Chuck and goodbye two-hundred dollars cash.

Extramarital affairs were rife at the motel. Those considered of great importance in both Summerside Hills and the neighboring town of MacLaughlin Springs were practically incestuous with one another. Judge Atwell, a man well into his sixties, regularly enjoyed the company of a young lady he introduced to Dean as Candy. Where he found her, Dean could only guess, but whenever the two arrived, usually once a week, their sexual appetites could be heard in intermittent bursts.

Even before Dean's tenure as manager, the Hill Side motel had garnered a reputation for the distasteful. A young man, the lover of a respected older woman on the town's select committee, was murdered in Room Thirteen. The body was discovered by the motel's cleaner and once the police arrived, the first officer to see the crime scene hurried from the room and promptly vomited. The young man had been castrated and his penis nailed to the ceiling above the bed. His testicles had been shoved into his mouth, his jaw pried apart with enough force to have snapped the mandible in three places. The culprit was never caught, though suspicion fell squarely on the committee member's husband, who was a prominent businessman rumoured to have ties with the same gang Chuck was a part of.

The motel had seen such things and much more, but when Dean Elton looked up from his cheap paperback to see a lone police officer strolling confidently toward the motel's reception, he knew he had nothing to hide today.

The officer came through the open door with an infectious smile that was enough of an initial distraction from the oddity of his sudden appearance. As he held out his hand to Dean, the manager noticed the fallacy behind the smile. He had met enough fake people in his time to sense bullshit and his bullshit radar had suddenly pinged into overdrive.

"Hi there!" said the Officer said enthusiastically. "How you doing today?"

Dean tentatively took the Officer's hand and shook it.

"As well as expected," he replied. "What can I do for you officer?"

"Oh, nothing much," the man replied, taking his hand back and casually wiping it on his pants, as if the act of touching Dean was filthy. "We've had an issue up at the nearby hospital and I was wondering if I could ask you a few questions, if I may?"

Hospital? Dean thought. Then it clicked.

"The quack house?" he asked.

The Officer's smile faltered. It was brief but Dean saw it, clear as day.

"We prefer the term hospital, if it's all the same, but yes, there was an attempted escape from the 'quack house' and we're asking around to see if anyone saw anything. Something suspicious maybe? Anything at all that may help us."

Dean frowned. Last he checked, the asylum was at least a twenty-minute drive outside of Summerside Hills. Why would the police be coming to his motel to ask questions about an escape? An *attempted* escape, which insinuated the situation was under control. Why would it be necessary for the police to question him?

Dean was not a stupid man. He glanced past the officer and

out toward the parking lot. There were no cruisers sitting idle. There were no cars there at all.

Did the cop walk all the way from town? Dean thought.

Unlikely.

He looked back at the officer and was surprised that he had not noticed just how unkempt the man was. His face was dirty, and his hair was matted and greasy.

"Can I see some ID please?" Dean asked.

That flicker again behind the smile.

"Of course," said the officer. "Give me a moment."

As the cop reached behind him with his left hand, his right came up with lightning speed and grabbed the motel manager by the hair. As Dean registered the sudden, painful pulling at his scalp, the cop yanked his head down and whacked it on the reception desk with alarming force. Stars flooded Dean's vision and as he tried to stand, the officer brought his head down a second and third time. The manager felt the man's fingers relinquish their grip, but his head spun relentlessly, and as he stood, he toppled backwards and collapsed behind the desk.

As the manager's eyes rolled back and his breathing became labored, Karl Molyneux calmly turned to the entrance, locked the door, and flipped the *Open* sign to *Closed*.

TWENTY-FIVE

Lucy was not lost, not physically at least, but her confrontation with Brandon had shocked her enough to question her role in their relationship. She needed space to think. As Brandon had walked toward the cars and the rest of the group, Lucy had turned and quietly walked away, unconsciously heading to the boat house where she knew she could remain undisturbed for a time to collect herself.

She had never seen Brandon react that way before, let alone toward her. He always seemed too keen to please that was one of the main attractions she had for him. Lucy had never wanted a vain man, though she was not blind to his strong arms and handsome face. Her attractions, however, were geared more toward a person's outlook, their wants in life, their aspirations. Their soul, as she would put it, and Brandon had a beautiful one. He was so earnest and caring and though he was not the first man to have adored Lucy, he was certainly the first man to show more than lust when he was with her. Though he would never admit it, and Lucy was oblivious of it, whenever Brandon looked at her, he could not believe his luck.

And now, with his outburst, Lucy had quickly come to realise how much she had taken his beautiful soul for granted.

She had always been a carefree personality and self-aware enough to know this. She was never one for planning, not rigidly at least, and if ever the opportunity for spontaneity arose, she seized it. Brandon, on the other hand, preferred structure over the impulsive, a plan for everything he did including his future. Lucy knew this going into their relationship of course, but it was always something she hoped she could change, to steer his behaviour to be more in line with hers.

Yet while he had always tried to accommodate her, it was only now that she fully realised she had seldom tried to accommodate his own desire for structure. And with that came guilt.

It was certainly not intentional, or intentionally malicious. In general Lucy considered herself a good person. She was always the one to make others feel comfortable, which was why she made a concerted effort with Gillian. How intimidating it must have been for the girl to be sat with a group of strangers, ones that already knew each other for many years. So, Lucy made the effort, spoke to her, went with her for food afterward, anything to put her at ease. Yet, when she thought about it, would she remain friends with Gillian once the summer was over? She honestly did not know, which, the more she thought about it, was unfair. Lucy was great at introductions but maintaining that connection with someone was usually effort she did not care for.

It was a wonder her relationship with Brandon had lasted as long as it had.

But she would be better, she promised herself. She would go to Brandon and apologise, sit and listen to him, if he still wanted her that was.

There was a word her mother always drilled into her, insufferably so, but now it seemed most apt for the issue at hand: Respect. She thought she had shown very little to Brandon, as if her mere presence was enough to maintain their relationship, but now she hoped she could give him the respect he wanted. She should have acknowledged his attempt at spontaneity when he had suggested they stay in Europe for longer than they had planned.

As she stood on the jetty opposite the boat house, she became aware that night had begun to creep in. Considering she had walked away unannounced, the others must be wondering where she was. She had no desire to return just yet, however, as she was sure she heard Marco shouting from the direction of the medical hut.

Best stay here, she thought. *They'll find me eventually, I'm sure.*

Lucy turned toward the lake and sat cross legged on the jetty. At least the evening air was warm and the ambience soothing.

Oh Brandon, she thought. *I'm so sorry.*

*

Dean Elton's breathing was unbearable, the kind of pig-snorting breaths a person does when they have been rendered temporarily unconscious, and as Karl Molyneux turned from the locked reception door, he brought his right foot down and crushed the manager's neck. There was an audible crunch as the man's throat collapsed, and as he wheezed, Karl brought it down again and again, until the wheezing ceased. He stood over the corpse and sized him up. Dean Elton was likely an inch or two taller than Karl and about twenty pounds heavier but better to steal clothes too big than squeeze into ones too small. The uniform Molyneux was wearing would only get him so far and by now the police would be watching for a lone officer. The sooner he changed the better.

To the right of the main reception desk was a room that was only marginally bigger than the guest rooms, with barely enough space for an old sofa bed, and stained, musty comforter. A small window above the headboard let in only a modicum of natural light. While there was a built-in closet like the other rooms, where they would normally be a bureau was a pile of dirty clothes, next to which was a camping stove. Where the man washed was not obvious to Karl.

He grabbed Dean's body by the feet and pulled him into the bedsit. He left the body on the floor and strolled to the closet where he was met with five sets of the same clothes. Luckily the proprietor did not appear to be a man with many friends. Besides it was getting dark now. All Karl had to do was blend in.

A knock at the reception door startled him. From where he

stood, he could not be seen from the main door.

He held his breath and waited.

The knocking continued.

"Dean?" came a raspy voice. "Dean, you in there?"

Molyneux crouched and edged his way forward, taking one of his stolen pistols from its holster and flicking the safety off.

"Damn, fool's probably drunk again," the man at the door said to himself, before Karl heard the *thump* of a heavy object being dropped outside. "Just the evening paper for you Dean," the man called. "I've left it outside the door with the bill. Don't be late with your payment again this time, ok?" There was silence, the interloper waiting for a reply that would never come. "Fuck him," the man muttered, before Karl heard footsteps retreating from the building.

Karl chanced a peek over the reception counter and saw the delivery man ride away on a bicycle. Standing, he saw the stack of evening papers laying to the right of the main entrance, tied neatly together, with his mugshot adorning the front page.

His eyes widened as he read the headline:

MOLYNEUX ESCAPES!
POLICE TO ENFORCE CURFEW UNTIL MURDERER
IS FOUND.

So, the public knew.

This will certainly complicate things, he thought.

★

The group prepared to find Lucy.

Conrad offered to join Brandon to the last place the two of them had been before the police arrived: the boat house. Gillian and Nick opted to search the three main dorm huts, starting with the one they had been headed to before being interrupted by the escaped patient. Chad and Trixie chose to search the area surrounding the shower block, and Stephen decided to stay and attempt to fix the thoroughly broken radio.

"Honestly think you can get it working?" Conrad had asked as Chad handed everyone flashlights and handheld radios.

Stephen had shrugged and said, "Who knows, but I can try. Otherwise, it's a very long hike back to civilisation in the morning."

Conrad nodded. "At least we have food and beds. As soon as we find Lucy, we'll dig out some tinned beans and bunker down for the night."

"If you say so boss."

"And the generators? Are they ready to go?"

"I've got the fuel loaded in the bed of my truck. I'll get 'em filled before you get back."

"Good man." Conrad looked at the group and asked, "Ready?"

They all nodded wearily. They were apprehensive.

"If you see anything untoward, and I mean *anything*, you alert us on the radio and you head straight back here. Understand?"

They nodded again.

SUMMERSIDE LAKE MASSACRE

That had been only five minutes before, yet Conrad and Brandon felt very much alone. Without the generators in use, the only light came from the flashlights they both held and the ever-dwindling glow from the central hub, which had its own power. The flashlights illuminated the path ahead perfectly, yet the woods around them were pitch black.

Conrad looked at Brandon.

"You ok son?" he asked.

"I just want to find her."

His boss smiled.

"We will."

*

Sheriff Douglas Clark received the update from David Edwards at the *Summerside Gazette* directly: the evening papers had gone out with the requested story. Doug was thankful and bid Edwards farewell, but not before the editor asked if the Sheriff had, had a chance to read the file he had lent him. Doug responded that he was getting to it and the two said their goodbyes.

That was half an hour prior and now, as he sat with his feet on his desk and a strong cup of coffee, Doug skimmed the file some more.

It was damning, that was for certain.

Their anonymous source, Waldo, was extraordinarily thorough. While there was much that could be dismissed as hearsay, the file did include photographs of Judge Atwell arriving at a seedy looking motel with a woman young enough to be his granddaughter. They appeared in good spirits, but the Judge's hands found their way up the woman's skirt and stayed there. They eventually disappeared into their room for what Doug could only assume was sex. There were many pictures such as these, mostly with the same woman, that had been taken at different times over the course of a year.

Waldo had also supplied bank statements, though how he had obtained them was a mystery to Doug. They consistently showed that, over many years, the Judge had been receiving additional payments from an undetermined source. They had started small but grown to be thousands of dollars extra a month. What was this money? Doug was sure those at the *Summerside Gazette* would speculate wildly but, should an investigation be mounted, the Sheriff was certain the source would be suspicious at best and criminal at worst. Might these payments have something to do with the Judge's insistence on having Molyneux transferred? If so, then part of the blame for their current plight could be laid at his door.

The Sheriff sipped his coffee and continued reading.

★

The killer had two of them in his sights. Tonight would be the night.

His attempt earlier that day had been foolhardy. He had not

waited patiently for almost a year, planned every detail and ensured the right people were hired to screw up on impulse. But he got greedy and struck early and it nearly cost him.

He would not get everyone of course. Rebecca's disappearing act last minute was unfortunate, but he could find her later. Patience, as they say, is a virtue, and the killer had a lot of it.

It was a shame about the black kid and his ginger friend. They were not part of his plan, but he could not leave any witnesses. Their silence would almost certainly guarantee his escape. Even with the best laid plans, collateral damage was to be expected.

No matter. Everything was now in place.

Yes, tonight would be the night.

TWENTY-SIX

C had went ahead with Trixie behind him, but both were tense. For Chad, it was a lifelong fear of the dark that he had yet to fully overcome. For Trixie, it was returning to the scene of that day's terror.

"So," said Chad, breaking the silence between them. "Marco huh?"

"What about Marco?" Trixie asked.

"Why him?"

Trixie shrugged as she stomped along behind him.

"It seemed like a good idea at the time," she said. "He was nice to me."

"He's nice to anyone he can use," said Chad. "And let me guess, now he's a piece of shit."

"It's his anger," Trixie said. "It overtakes him, you know?"

"Oh, I know," said Chad. "I saw him start on a kid that *he* walked into once. Just beat the hell out of him. Poor kid didn't know what the hell was going on or why."

Trixie nodded. She knew what that kid felt.

"He has some good traits," she offered.

"Kinda sounds like you're defending him."

There was a sudden *thump* against Chad's arm that made him yell. He quickly turned to see Trixie with her fists clenched, looking fiercely angry.

"Did you just *hit* me?" Chad shouted.

"I am *not* defending him!" Trixie shouted back. "Do you know what he would do if he even *thought* the two of us were talking right now?"

She lifted her top enough to show a faint but noticeable bruise on her abdomen. Passing her flashlight over it showed its extent.

Chad stared, shocked.

"He did that to you?" he whispered.

Trixie nodded.

"I laughed at something funny," she said. "He thought I was laughing at him, so he shoved me against a wall. Hard." She pulled her top back down.

"What an asshole," said Chad. "I'm sorry that happened to you."

"Why you apologising? It wasn't you that did it."

"Even so, no one should be treated like that."

"Well," Trixie said hesitantly. She was not used to niceties, especially from a boy. "It's not like I can walk away."

"What do you mean?"

"You serious?" she asked as Chad looked at her sincerely. "Because he'll hurt me even *worse*. The minute I tell him it's over is the day I wind up in hospital being fed through tubes." She let out an involuntary laugh. "Chad, you're cute, but you can be *so* simple."

Chad raised an eyebrow.

"You think I'm cute?" he asked.

Trixie rolled her eyes.

"Whatever. C'mon, we're nearly there," she said as she brushed past him.

★

Lucy heard approaching footsteps from the woods to the side of the boathouse. She turned, hoping to see Brandon and expecting to at least see *someone*, yet there was no-one in sight.

"Brandon?" she called as she stood. "Is that you?"

From behind the boat house she noticed two beams of torch light. She smiled.

"Lucy?" came a familiar voice.

"Brandon!" she called and ran toward the lights, her heart lifting.

"Conrad! She's here! She's by the…what are you doing?"

Lucy stopped dead as a scream of agony issued from her boyfriend. The cries emanating from Brandon from the unseen attack made her blood run cold.

"Get off him!" Conrad shouted over Brandon's screams.

SUMMERSIDE LAKE MASSACRE

Lucy snapped out of her shock and sprinted toward the uproar as Conrad began to yell also. As she approached, the screams were accompanied by a wet thumping sound not unlike a steak being tenderised.

"Brandon!" Lucy shrieked as she rounded the corner of the boat house.

The sight that met her was appalling.

Brandon was on his back with multiple stab wounds to his abdomen. His blue shirt was maroon with the volume of blood flowing from him and the ground beneath him was sodden. The damage to his body was unbearable for Lucy to comprehend. His assailant had unleashed a flurry of attacks in barely any time at all with the sole purpose of ending Brandon's life as brutally as possible.

Embedded within his neck was an arrow, the kind used for the camp's archery lessons.

Lucy froze. How could she when she had barely processed that violence before her?

Conrad was nowhere to be seen.

Brandon spluttered. He practically vomited blood.

Lucy knelt beside him and placed her hands around the arrow in her boyfriend's neck in an attempt to stem some of the bleeding. The fact that he was still alive was a miracle and Lucy clung onto whatever hope there would be of him surviving.

"Don't move!" she said, panicked. "Try not to move! Oh Jesus!"

Her hands grew slick with his blood and as Brandon

spluttered more, her clothes and her face were hit with spray. She stared down at him and saw fear in his eyes, true fear, the kind one feels when met with their own mortality.

Brandon reached for her cheek, gingerly stroking her face with his bloodied fingers before his face went slack. Lucy saw his pupils widen as he died.

Lucy stared in disbelief. The full comprehension of what she had witnessed eluded her. The night before she and Brandon had shared cheeseburgers with Nick and the new girl. They had walked home arm in arm and fell asleep watching movies on the couch. In what world would she ever imagine watching her boyfriend die so bloodily before her?

Coming to her senses, what was left of them, she heard further commotion in the trees ahead. As she looked up, numb, she made out the unmistakable sound of Conrad's voice.

He was in distress.

She squinted into the darkness yet there was no sign of him. Whoever had attacked them had either chased Conrad or been chased by him into the surrounding trees. Whatever the circumstances, it would seem Conrad was close to his own death if she did not move.

The screaming stopped. The silence was deafening.

"Conrad?" she called gingerly as every fibre of her being yelled for her to run.

There was a *whoosh* of something passing her head before feeling a sting in her cheek. She lifted her hand to her face and winced. Something had cut her cheek open.

SUMMERSIDE LAKE MASSACRE

The second *whoosh* hit her.

Lucy stumbled back as the wind was knocked out of her, pain radiating from her right shoulder. She looked down to find an arrow identical to the one in her boyfriend's corpse embedded in her.

As a third arrow missed her Lucy finally found her voice and screamed. She forgot Conrad, forgot Brandon, forgot the arrow that was stuck in her. She screamed loudly and hysterically before running toward central green.

As she sprinted, the trees silently watched as the killer followed.

*

Deputy Elias Ansel barely had time to swerve as the woman darted into the road.

He was as good as his word to the Sheriff and had continued to patrol Molyneux's last known whereabouts in some vague hope that he may just happen to see him.

His mind had begun to wonder when the woman dressed in a hospital gown waved manically for him to stop.

The fact that he saw her at all was a miracle. Night had crept in quickly and the new moon gave off no additional light. All Elias had was the flashlight in the passenger seat and the high beams of his cruiser.

His reactions were impressive and as soon as he noticed the flicker of movement, he brought the cruiser to a hard right and pressed both feet on the brake. To the right of the road was a ditch, and no amount of braking could fight against gravity. The cruiser tipped forward and down. Elias had a moment to see the incoming bank before the engine block collided with the ground. The strength of the impact was sudden, and the abrupt tug against his seat belt forced the wind out of him.

Dazed, Deputy Ansel took stock of his surroundings. The car was still, but its angle was steep. There would be no way of driving out and besides, the steam pouring from the engine was all Elias needed to see the damage was irreparable. Elias began to reach for the radio before noticing it in several pieces in the passenger footwell. The impact had shunted it from its place on the dashboard.

"Shit," Elias muttered to himself.

"Hello?" came a timid voice from behind the cruiser.

The Deputy gently undid his seat belt and kicked open the driver's side door. His ungraceful exit from the cruiser was accompanied by a drop of a few feet. Despite the heat of the last couple of days, the ditch Elias landed in was sodden and he sank to his ankles in a mix of mud and stagnant water. He cursed himself before seeing a flicker of movement above him.

The woman was stood at the top of the bank.

"Are you ok?" she asked.

Elias instinctively rested his hand on his service weapon yet hesitated when the woman flinched. Despite the darkness, he could make out her shape and her unkempt appearance. It was the hospital gown, however, that the Deputy recognised.

"Annette Maxwell?" he asked tentatively.

The woman frantically looked from side to side, as if scared others may arrive. She then looked back at Elias and nodded.

The Deputy relaxed a little. He had read her file earlier. She was considered relatively harmless compared to others at Lake Side. He had yet to lift his hand from his gun, however.

"Are you going to be a problem?" he asked.

Annette shook her head and said, "I just," she sobbed, "I just want to go home."

"I'm going to lift my hand away from my weapon, ok?" said Elias. He spread his fingers wide and slowly moved his hand from his hip. He could see the patient's shoulders slump as tension left her.

"Now," said the Deputy, sheepishly. "Can you help me up?"

*

Stephen turned as he heard Lucy's screams.

He hurried out the medical hut to see her sprinting into the central green. She was a sight of horror. She was bloody from head to toe and in a state of hysteria, but it was the arrow in her shoulder that caused alarm in Stephen.

"Help me!" she screamed, her terror emphasising her plea.

Stephen did not stop to think. He ran toward her ready to carry her to the medical hut and tend to her wounds. To see someone so young in such distress appalled him.

As he reached her Lucy threw herself at him and began to

sob. They collapsed on the ground together, Stephen clutching the frightened girl.

"What is it?" he yelled over her sobs.

"They killed Brandon!" she cried.

Stephen opened his mouth to say something when Lucy was struck in the head from behind. The arrow penetrated her skull with ease and passed through the tissue of her brain and out her left eye socket almost instantly.

Stephen recoiled in horror as her body went limp, her left eye dangling in shredded tatters from the arrowhead. As he scrambled away from the corpse, he let out his own hysterical scream.

It was then that a shiny object approached him at speed from the direction Lucy had come and struck him in his ankle.

He yelled as his leg gave out from under him. He stared down at his ankle and turned pale.

The arrow had hit him in his right leg where the shin met his foot, piercing perfectly through the joint and exiting where his achilleas tendon should have been. The tendon itself was severed and the wound pulsed as his leg continued and failed to pump blood into his foot.

He sat up and pulled his foot toward him, hissing through the pain. The arrow had stopped with only its head exposed above his heel, leaving most of the arrow's length below his shin. He grasped what protruded with both hands, held his breath, and snapped the wood in half.

The pain was not as fierce as he expected yet the experience was not any less uncomfortable. The real test, however, would be removing the arrowhead.

Blood still flowed from the exit wound and as Stephen mustered up the courage to pull what remained of the arrow from his ankle, panic settled in. Regardless of how successful he was at removing the arrowhead he would still be unable to place any weight on his leg.

Stephen inhaled and clutched the arrowhead. *Like ripping off a band-aid,* he thought.

The metal of the arrowhead dug into the skin of his palm as he pulled what remained of the arrow through his leg. The sensation was appalling. He did not stop and, despite the pain, he yanked the arrow with force and speed until it was free.

Stephen screamed. A series of spasms shot up his leg as he held the final half of the arrow in his bloodied hand. He stared at the offending piece of wood and threw it in the direction from where it had come.

His assailant, who had been watching the Janitor struggle, strolled from the shadows. An apparition intent on violence marched forward wearing the uniform for the Clark family lumber mill, their face obscured by a jet-black ski mask.

With both hands, the man carried a fire axe.

Stephen's panic intensified as he turned on his front and hurriedly crawled away. The medical hut was no more than fifty feet from him, yet it could not have been further away. He had been reduced to a pathetic belly crawl as he heard his pursuer approaching. Stephen risked a look behind him and rolled onto his back, watching as Death approached.

"Please," Stephen said, "please, don't!"

The attacker continued his march.

Stephen shoved himself backward, his working heel sliding into the soft soil for purchase.

"Please, you don't have to do this!" he shrieked.

His attacker was only ten paces from him. The man tensed, grabbed the base of the axe with both hands, brought it up over his head, and swung it down with terrifying power.

The blade struck the shin of Stephen's intact leg with enough force to break the bone. The blade itself was not sharp, so Its journey through the leg was ragged and messy. It did not slice through his flesh so much as rip it, through skin, muscle, and ligaments, before the blade embedded itself with a dull *thud* into the soil.

In less than a second, a quarter of Stephen's leg was removed, and he stared in horror as shock hit him. Adrenaline caused his whole body to shake and as he struggled to come to terms with the sheer brutality of the violence enacted upon him, the attacker pulled the axe free, held it in both hands and stared down at the whimpering caretaker.

Stephen looked his killer in the eye and raised his hands in a feeble, pleading gesture.

The attacker lifted his mask. The lights outside the medical hut were enough for Stephen to make out a wicked smile.

"You!" Stephen gasped.

The killer nodded.

"But…but why?" Stephen asked.

The killer answered by stepping forward and resting his foot on Stephen's bloody stump. The agony was relentless and the only noise the caretaker could muster was a large intake of breath as air fled him. Tears streamed his face, from pain and self-pity, and he mustered the energy to stare his attacker in the eye one last time. He showed no defiance, just disbelief that his life would end in such a heinous fashion.

"Please," he asked again.

The killer raised the axe over his head a final time.

"*No!*" screamed Stephen as he held up his arm in an attempt to block the attack. For just the briefest of moments he witnessed the axe slice through his arm as messily as it had his leg, before it embedded itself in his face.

At that moment Stephen ceased to care about very much at all.

TWENTY-SEVEN

The more he read, the more mortified he became.

That snake, thought the Sheriff.

Judge Atwell's unsavoury deeds went way back. For more than thirty years he had accepted payments of all kinds to ensure outcomes favourable to whoever paid. These included prioritising the building of new homes despite environmental concerns, sentencing people thought to be undesirable to harsher prison terms than was considered normal for their crimes, to even declaring some mentally unfit and damning them to a life at Lake Side hospital for treatment they did not need. All for the purpose of lining his pockets.

What was extraordinary, though, were the names of those that were complicit. While the information the Sheriff had would be considered circumstantial, there was enough for an investigation that would see heads roll.

Whoever this Waldo guy was, Doug Clark wanted to shake

their hand.

Clark turned the page to find a messily annotated list of names on the headed paper for Lake Side hospital. A full third of the names had been underlined and a handwritten note in the margin read:

These are the names of patients I suspect Judge Atwell, with the help of ex-Sheriff Wydell and the late warden Brett Martin, incarcerated at Lake Side against their will.

Douglas skimmed through the names, and while there were some he recognised, having been responsible for their initial arrests, there was one that leaped off the page light a firecracker.

Now that's a remarkable coincidence, he thought.

The name, Annette Maxwell, was underlined more than the others, as if it held particular significance.

*

"Water."

Elias was admiring the filth that was now drying around his feet when the woman spoke.

Though the night was warm, Annette Maxwell hugged herself. She had helped him up from the ditch with surprising strength. It was only then that she noticed just how thirsty she was.

"Water," she repeated.

"I don't have any I'm afraid," Elias replied. "And we can't drive anywhere to get any."

He stared down at his cruiser and frowned.

"What the hell were you doing anyway, running out like that? I could've hit you."

"I just...I don't know," said Annette. She stared up at him with desperate, pleading eyes.

"I don't know what to do," she said, sobbing lightly. "I just want to go home."

"The hospital?" asked Elias.

Annette shook her head.

"Home," she repeated. "With my mom and dad."

Elias stared.

"Your mom and dad?" he asked. "I'm sorry but I read they both passed away years back."

Annette's face went white.

"What!" she exclaimed. "But my Pa's only turning fifty!"

The Deputy watched her and was taken by just how child like her mannerisms were. The way she hugged herself, the upward inflection at the end of each sentence, even the way she tucked he hair behind her ears. She was like a teenager trapped in an older woman's body.

"Ma'am, what year do you think it is?"

Maxwell's confusion grew. No one had ever asked her that and she had never thought to find out. How long had she been a resident at Lake Side? All sense of time and place had disappeared but that was not to say she was totally unaware of herself.

What was the last thing she remembered? Fully remembered, before Lake Side?

Summer. Yes, and the heat and trees and wooden huts. And a lake? Sure, a lake, bright and clear and refreshing on those hot summer days.

And the men. The bad men. The men that had hurt her.

She had looked young then. So young and innocent.

The memories were still fragmented but the dread they stirred hit her like a gut shot.

Her breathing became heavy.

The Deputy stood before her and placed his arms on her shoulders.

"Woah, easy there," he said. "Look at me."

She looked at him.

"You're safe ok?" he continued. "I'll make sure you're safe. You can trust me."

Can I? She thought. It had been such a long time since she trusted anyone.

"Sixty-five," Annette said.

"Ma'am?"

"The year," she said. "It must be nineteen sixty-five."

Though he tried to hide it, the shock on the Deputy's face must have been obvious.

"Isn't it?" Annette asked desperately.

"Oh man," said Elias quietly. "What did they do to you?"

★

Across Camp Summerside, Stephen Haig's death cries echoed through the trees.

Trixie and Chad had made it back to the shower block, and Nick and Gillian had already searched one of the three dormitories when they heard the screams. All four stopped dead and whipped their heads in the direction of the central green as a terrible, sinking horror enveloped them like ice.

★

"What the hell?"

Gillian felt a strong clamp on her upper arm and looked down to find Nick was clutching her for dear life.

"Careful, would you?" she said, pulling her arm away.

"Did you hear that?" Nick asked frantically.

"Of course I heard it!" said Gillian. "It was probably heard it in town!"

"What the hell was it?"

"How the hell am I supposed to know?"

"What do we do?" asked Nick.

A good question, though Gillian had no desire to investigate what had caused such a gut-wrenching cry. She also did not want to be out in the dark with only one other person. She trusted

Nick, but they would be better protected as a group.

"We need to find the others," Gillian said. She took the radio from her waistband and pressed the call button.

"Guys? What's happening?"

Silence.

She pressed call again and said, "This really isn't funny. Did any of you hear that scream? Is everyone ok? Can everyone call in please?"

Silence.

"Piece of shit!" she yelled and hit it with the palm of her hand. When no response came, she took Nick by the hand. "C'mon," she said as she started to lead them toward the shower hut in the hope that Chad and Trixie were still there.

★

The area around the shower hut and latrines was far too dark. Stephen had obviously yet to turn on the additional generators that powered the lighting for rest of the camp. Yet as the man's final pleas for his life crashed through the surrounding area, both Chad and Trixie became all too aware of the darkness around them.

"That sounded like Stephen!" said Chad in a state of shock. "What the hell is happening over there?"

He took a step toward the path back before Trixie grabbed him by the arm.

"Don't go," she said.

"What?"

"Please don't go."

Chad frowned.

"He could be in danger!" he said in protest.

Trixie nodded.

"He could be, but we're safer if we stay here."

"Are you serious?"

Trixie bit her lips nervously and nodded again.

"I don't believe this," said Chad, frustrated.

"I'm scared, alright!" yelled Trixie. "So, sue me! With everything that's been happening, I'm not overly keen to run toward danger."

Chad sighed and grabbed the radio clipped to his belt buckle.

"Anyone there? This is Chad." He held the radio to his ear and waited.

There was a short burst of feedback followed by heavy breathing.

"Chad?" came a female voice.

"That you Lucy?" Chad asked.

"It's Gillian," came the reply. *"Where are you guys?"*

"We're at the shower block. Did you hear the scream?"

"Who didn't?"

"I'm going to investigate," said Chad. "Trixie will wait for you here ok?"

"You're going alone?"

Chad thought for a moment and realised how foolhardy his decision may be. He was unarmed and there were many things that had happened that day none of them fully understood.

But Stephen had been kind to Chad, more so than his own father. To abandon him at a time of need almost felt like a betrayal.

"I'll be ok," he said.

"Wait for us," Gillian said.

"It might be too late by then," Chad replied and shut his radio off.

He rested a hand on Trixie's shoulder and said, "Wait for them. I'll be right back." He smiled reassuringly before turning and sprinting in the direction of the central green, leaving Trixie alone in the dark.

★

"Well, the radio in my cruiser's busted," said Deputy Ansel. "But I know this road. There's a motel not far from here. You ok to walk? I can call the Sheriff from there."

Annette Maxwell nodded.

Elias smiled and said, "I'm sure there's food you can have while we're there too. Maybe some warmer clothes. Just don't run ok? I'm here to help you. You believe that don't you?"

Annette paused for a moment before nodding.

"Excellent," said the Deputy. "Let's get moving."

TWENTY-EIGHT

Karl Molyneux checked the ledger at reception and was happy to see the motel was empty of guests. There were none expected for at least two more days when the summer season began. He could lay low here for some time before further attempting to leave town. It also meant he had the pick of any room he desired, so he opted for the honeymoon suite. He found the idea of bathing in a heart-shaped bath to be utterly hilarious.

He walked to the owner's bedsit and pulled one of the identical sets of clothes from the closet and checked the sizes. Both the shirt and the pants would be a size too big but it they were better than nothing.

He removed the dirty police shirt and was in the process of removing the stolen gun belt when he heard voices outside.

★

SUMMERSIDE LAKE MASSACRE

Chad arrived at the central green to find it empty except for one item at its centre. The lights were dimmer than he would have liked and he was acutely aware of the darkness around him, though there was enough to show the large dark patch on the grass where the item lay.

He cautiously approached, surveying the area.

"Stephen?" he called. While he had no weapon, he took solace in how open the central green was. He would have time to react should he be approached.

"Stephen, it's Chad," he called again.

The only response was the creaking of the trees.

A sinking feeling enveloped him. Though the surrounding bulbs gave a light orange hue to the area, the dark patch of grass appeared to glisten and reflect a color Chad hoped not to see.

He shone his flashlight in the direction of the mess.

Red. Deep, crimson red.

And as Chad drew even closer, he was able to determine just what it was at the centre of that darkness. It was enough to cause his stomach to lurch and for him to retch.

It was one of Stephen's sneakers. His severed foot was still in it.

Chad took a step forward and felt a *squelch* under his shoe. He lifted his foot to find a shredded eyeball stuck to the sole.

Chad screamed and frantically wiped the offending thing from his shoe before he promptly turned from both eye and dismembered foot and vomited.

He did not see the man in the lumber uniform watching him

from the medical hut window.

★

Trixie was afraid and conflicted.

She did not want to follow Chad, yet by staying where she was she had allowed herself to be alone and more vulnerable. Gillian and Nick would arrive soon but, without the lights on, the dark was significant. Her mind wandered and conjured all manner of unseen horrors just waiting to kill her, all out of reach from her flashlight's beam. It was foolish, she admitted, yet she could not help herself.

Trixie heard footsteps behind her. They advanced confidently, not quietly. Not the approach of a would-be killer.

Gillian, she thought, and smiled.

"Oh, thank god you're here," she said and turned.

The person grabbed her forcibly by the hair, yanked her head back, and rammed it hard against the outside wall of the shower hut. Trixie saw stars and became dizzy, stumbling backwards from her attacker and falling on her backside. She stared up at the figure whose shadow loomed over her like impending death.

She instinctively reached up to her forehead and felt warm, sticky blood.

Though the dark obscured her attacker's face, she could see their shoulders bobbing as they laughed.

"Where's your pretty boy now, bitch?" said Marco.

★

SUMMERSIDE LAKE MASSACRE

From Stephen's severed foot was a trail of blood and torn up grass that lead to the medical hut. Should Stephen be alive, he had either dragged himself, or been dragged in that direction.

Chad took a step forward and stopped. While it was possible that Mr Haig was alive, another seed had planted itself and began to grow with a fury, one that Chad kicked himself for not assuming sooner.

Unless the man had stood in a bear trap, there was no way the wound was accidental. It all made sense when the events of the day were considered. The sabotage of the car engines and the radio, Trixie and Marco's bizarre encounter at the shower hut, the sudden appearance of the escaped mental patient, Lucy's disappearance, and now this. Someone had hateful intent on the group, and Chad suddenly felt that he was too far out of his depth to even confront such a menace.

He also felt thoroughly alone and vulnerable.

Should've waited for the others, he thought.

A loud *thump* from the medical hut broke his contemplation.

It could be Stephen. It could also be the attacker.

"Who's there?" he yelled.

He was met with silence.

"Whoever's in there, come out now!" Chad could only hope that he sounded more menacing than he felt.

The door to the medical hut opened.

Beyond the open doorway the interior of the hut was a void of darkness. Chad half expected someone, be it Stephen, the assailant, *anyone*, to emerge from the void as if exiting a different realm.

Chad waited. There was the ambience of the lake gently lapping against the shore, the wind through the trees, and the distant hum of the central generators, yet no one emerged from the hut.

"This is your last chance!" he shouted. "Come out now and we can deal with this, man to man!"

No one answered. The hut door remained open.

Chad inhaled deeply and tentatively followed the trail of blood while clutching his flashlight.

★

"What's the matter? Can't talk?"

Trixie shimmied backward as Marco stepped forward. The smile on his face was delirious. It chilled Trixie to the bone. She had never seen such mania in him before.

"Marco-" she began.

"That's me. You remember your man, don't you?" he said before kicking her in her right thigh. She yelled in pain as he continued to loom over her.

"Think you're clever, huh bitch?" Marco said, kicking her again. His foot connected with her abdomen and she folded inward. "Lover boy leave you alone did he? That's a shame. You could really use his help right now couldn't you?"

"Please," she said, wheezing. "Please leave me alone."

"We're just talking babe," said Marco, kicking dirt in her

face. "Didn't you always say we should talk more? Well, I'll talk, you listen.

"You drive me crazy, you know that?" he continued. "Every fuckin' day we're together, you're bustin' my balls about *everything*. You're like a broken record. Nothin' I do is ever good enough. But I'm not about to take that kind of shit from you. That's why I do it you know? You gotta know your place sometimes, and what's a little slapping around between lovers huh? You shut up when I smack you. It works. But then you forget, so I gotta smack you around some more. It's exhaustin' really. You ever think about that? How tirin' it is being with you? But you forgot the *one* rule about dating me."

He squatted beside Trixie, grabbed the front of her t-shirt, and pulled her close enough that she could smell his cigarette tainted breath.

"Remember what that rule was?" he asked. "You *don't fuck with Marco!*"

As he bought his free hand back and clenched his fist, Trixie grabbed a handful of dirt, as much as she could, and pressed it against her boyfriend's eyes. Marco screamed as grit and grass scratched his eyeballs. He quickly let go of Trixie and frantically strained to wipe as much muck from his face as possible. The more he blinked the worse it became as dirt found its way underneath his eyelids.

Trixie pushed away, brought up her right leg and kicked Marco in his abdomen, pushing him onto the balls of his feet, where he lost balance and fell backwards. He flailed around in pain as the stinging in his eyes continued.

Trixie stood, the left side of her face covered in blood and dirt and looked down at the sight of her boyfriend. Anger over came her like she had never known. She gritted her teeth and let out a shrill scream as she brought up her foot and stomped on Marco's testicles. He screamed in return and began retching.

"I have had!" stomp *"enough!"* stomp *"Of YOU!"*

Her heel connected with enough force for something to crunch underfoot. Marco vomited as he bucked in unbelievable pain. Trixie laughed. It was exhilarating to see him so pathetic, so *emasculated*. She snorted, hocking up a load of phlegm that she spat at his face.

Breathing heavily, she looked up to see Gillian and Nick stood a short distance away, their mouths agape. Nick held a rock over his head.

Marco continued to cry at Trixie's feet.

"Jesus," was all Gillian could say.

"Was that for me?" Trixie asked Nick, breathless, pointing at the rock he was holding.

"What?" he said before realising he was still stood with it raised. "Oh, this. It was for Marco actually."

"How long have you guys been stood there?" Trixie asked.

"Since you blinded him," said Gillian, her face ashen. "After that it didn't look like you needed help."

Trixie nodded and smiled. As she stepped over Marco and toward her friends, the whimpering figure reached for her in a futile gesture of attack. She stepped on his wrist, causing Marco to cry out again, and continued on without breaking a stride.

"Where's Chad?" asked Nick.

"He went off ahead," Trixie said. "C'mon, we need to find him."

★

The sign on the door to the motel reception read *Closed*, which seemed odd to Elias, though the inconvenience was minor. Should it come to it he could break the glass and let himself in. He would be reprimanded for sure, but the Sheriff's department would pay for any damage.

He told Annette to stand back, then he tapped lightly on the door.

"Hello? Anyone there?"

Nothing.

He tapped again, harder this time.

"My name is Deputy Elias Ansel of the Sheriff's department," he called loudly. "I need to use your phone. If there is anyone here, please open the door or I will be forced to break in."

Still nothing.

The Deputy shrugged. He looked over at Annette and smiled.

"Stay back," he said, unbuckling his pistol. "I've always wanted to do this."

Elias checked the safety catch was on. No need for a misfire while also breaking and entering. It did not occur to him to use his flashlight for such a task.

He grabbed his pistol by the barrel and, wielding it like a hammer, smashed it against the top glass pane of the door. The whole thing shattered and came crashing down, scattering shards of glass across the reception floor. In the quiet ambience of the motel the noise was practically deafening. Annette covered her ears and let out short yelp.

As the cacophony settled, Elias reached through the door and unlocked the latch with a *snick*. He had rested his hand on the inside door handle and began to push when he noticed the topless man standing in the doorway to the right of the reception desk.

"Oh!" said Elias, startled. "I'm sorry, I didn't realise anyone was-"

Karl Molyneux raised one of his stolen pistols, aimed it at the deputy, and fired.

TWENTY-NINE

Wilbur Donnington sat on his porch and grew concerned. It was unlike Dean to miss evening beers. Even with the amount he drank in the day he always arrived at 8pm like clockwork, as if the act was hardwired into his DNA.

Yet as 9pm had come and gone, Wilbur's friend was nowhere to be seen.

Wilbur stood, stretched his old bones, and decided he would march right over to the motel and check on Dean himself. The light from that god-awful neon sign was visible from Wilbur's house. All he had to do was walk down the road that ran from his house to the treeline of his property and onto the main road. It was only a further hundred metres from there in a straight line to the motel.

As he placed his straw hat upon his head, he heard a car skidding as it lost control, then a crash.

He tentatively stayed on his porch, unsure whether to call the police or investigate.

"Wilbur!" came his wife's voice from inside the house.

"Yeah!"

"What's that racket!?"

"Just some idiot crashing their car, honey!"

"On that road?" his wife said. "How the hell do you do that?"

"I don't know sweetie! Try go back to sleep!"

There was a mumbling from the house that he barely heard, then nothing. Vera apparently had nothing left to say.

Wilbur reached into his pocket and pulled out a tin of chewing tabaco. He removed the lid, grabbed a clump, and tucked it into his mouth. He listened for anything further on the road. It was quite rare to see and accident on that road. You could see for miles ahead of you, even at dusk.

Must've hit an elk, Wilbur thought. *Only thing that makes sense.*

He had turned to the front door with the intention of grabbing another beer and calling the motel to check on Dean when he heard the unmistakable rapport of gunfire.

Wilbur Donnington would be calling the police after all.

★

Chad held his flashlight as a club as he entered the medical hut, its beam illuminating the chilling, stark space before him.

His ingrained habit would be to turn to the right and enter

the office, however something on his left under the hut's solitary bed caught his eye. It was barely visible in the dark.

He turned his flashlight to the bed and was immediately met with sight of two legs sticking out from underneath. The rest of the body was obscured by the mattress.

Chad's heart pounded ferociously as he approached the body. The closer he got, the more glaringly obvious it became that this was not Stephen. The body had both feet.

Chad crouched to find Lucy laying under the bed like discarded trash. The arrow was still in her head, and Chad's stomach turned at the memory of the eyeball, Lucy's eyeball, squelching under his foot.

He put a hand to his mouth and held back tears. First Stephen, and now Lucy. It was only then that he remembered of Conrad and Brandon. Where were they? Were they safe?

The killer silently stepped from the office, through the doorway and moved toward him.

*

Trixie, Gillian and Nick arrived at the main green to find it deserted save for the same grotesque sight that had greeted Chad. Though Nick squinted, Gillian gasped at the sight of the severed appendage. Trixie stared. Her confrontation with Marco seemed to have drained her of any emotion, though, much like Gillian, she let out a short cry of horror.

"Chad!" Gillian shouted.

There was no reply.

"What are you doing?!" hissed Nick. "Whoever did this might still be here!"

"You sure he came this way?" Gillian asked Trixie, hurriedly.

"A hundred percent," Trixie replied. Her gaze followed the trails of blood and dirt to the open door of the medical hut. She took a step forward before Nick placed a hand gently on her arm.

"What are you doing?" he asked, scared.

"Going to see if he's in there," said Trixie, frowning at him.

"We don't know if he's in there," Nick continued.

"No, we don't," said Trixie, "but we won't know if we don't look. Besides, he went alone because *I* was too scared. I *have* to find him."

Nick pulled back and looked sheepishly at his feet. Gillian placed a hand on his shoulder and nodded at Trixie.

"At least let us come with you," Gillian said. "We'll be safer if we're-"

There was the sound of someone stumbling out of the medical hut. The three of them looked up to see Chad stood in the doorway looking deathly pale.

"Chad!" Trixie cried, smiling. She began to run toward him when he stumbled down the short set of stairs just outside the door. He was clutching his side and as Trixie stopped, horror filling her, she noticed the knife embedded to the hilt in Chad's side. Behind her, Gillian and Nick screamed as a figure emerged from the darkness of the hut and into the doorway. Trixie noticed the killer's uniform was covered in blood, far more than was possible from one person, and glistened like a newly glossed wall.

He knelt next to Chad's prone form and slowly removed the knife, relishing the cries of anguish from his dying victim. The others stared in horror. The killer did not take his eyes off them. He plunged the knife back into Chad before drawing it across his stomach. As his victim coughed blood, the wound at his middle opened and his guts spilled out over the grass at the hut's entrance.

His friends could only stare in horror.

As Chad died, the killer stood and smiled, wiping the fresh blood from the knife onto his pants.

Gillian and Nick turned and bolted toward the main hall with Trixie close behind them. Nick arrived first and slammed into the door, which was unlocked, sending him sprawling forward as Gillian followed him. Her feet hit Nick and she too fell forward, too fast to react in time, and hit the wooden floor with her temple.

"Wait for me!" screamed Trixie as she approached.

Nick turned from where he lay and shook Gillian's shoulders. He reeled in shock to see the large headwound that was steadily pumping blood. Trixie's screams quickly registered, and he pushed Gillian off him with all his strength.

"WAIT FOR ME!" Trixie screamed again as Nick lunged at the door.

The killer was directly behind his prey.

Trixie dove through the open door as Nick slammed it

closed, pushing his full weight behind it. The knife connected with the wood with a dull *thud*, its tip penetrating all the way and missing Nick's eye by millimetres as the door latch clicked into place. There was a sudden rattle as the killer hit the door with his shoulder, sending Nick staggering back.

The killer barged against the door a second time, harder than the first. Trixie scrambled to her feet, oblivious to Gillian's unconscious form, reached up and bolted the interior locks.

The crash happened a third time before the killer attempted the door handle to no avail. He yelled with fury as he repeatedly kicked the door. The wood continued to rattle, the hinges squeaked, but it remained sturdy. It would take a lot more for it to break. There was another howl in anger before the blade of the knife suddenly retracted. Both Nick and Trixie remained silent and listened tentatively as the killer's footsteps retreated.

Nick let out a sigh of relief.

"Is he gone?" he asked.

"Maybe," said Trixie. "Or he's getting something better to break the door down."

"Great," said Nick before turning to check on Gillian. He stopped dead and screamed. He heard Trixie let out her own terrified cry as she saw what awaited them in the centre of the main hall.

Hanging from the ceiling by a noose was the mangled body Stephen Haig, his foot missing as well as his left hand, his head split open. Underneath him was a congealing patch of blood that had leaked from his wounds. At the patch's centre was a head they immediately recognised.

It belonged to Wallace Asher.

Written around it in blood was one word:

COMPLICIT

THIRTY

The Sheriff was drifting off to sleep at his desk when the phone rang. It nearly sent him toppling backward off his chair. He grabbed the receiver and rubbed his eyes.

"Sheriff Clark," he grumbled.

"Doug, it's Wiley," said the Lieutenant. "We've got reports of gun fire at Lake Side motel, outside of town. I'm heading there now."

Gunfire? Thought the Sheriff, before remembering what Deputy Ansel had said to him earlier that evening, that he would patrol the streets a little while longer.

Molyneux! He's found him!

"I'm on my way," said the Sheriff, and hung up before the Lieutenant could respond.

★

SUMMERSIDE LAKE MASSACRE

The bullet clipped Deputy Ansel's ear and sent him spiralling to the right as a second bullet whizzed over his head. He landed on his right side and felt a small *crack* as he hit the concrete. There was pain in his shoulder and elbow, but he could not worry about that now.

Dazed, he rolled onto his back and groped for his weapon as Molyneux appeared over the reception desk and fired again. The bullet nicked the concrete next to Elias's head. He pulled his weapon free and returned fire.

Molyneux ducked behind the counter as the Deputy's own rounds struck the desk and the wall behind him, sending splinters and plaster dust flying around the reception. The bedlam ceased only when Ansel's gun ran dry.

Elias kept his weapon pointed toward his target as he stood. He chanced a quick glimpse toward Annette, who was cowering by the door to room 1.

"Stay down!" he yelled at Maxwell before returning his attention to the motel's reception.

"Karl Molyneux!" shouted Elias. "Stand up and show me your hands!"

"Or what?" Molyneux shouted back. His tone was almost jovial.

"Or I'll shoot you!" the Deputy replied.

"Oooh I'm shaking," Molyneux said sarcastically. "Sorry buddy, but that ain't happening."

He fired a flurry of bullets blindly over the reception desk, causing Elias to go prone. He heard the whizz of ammunition flying past him as he glanced and heard Molyneux's gun run empty.

"Fuck!" he heard the psychopath exclaim.

The Deputy did not hesitate. He swiftly reloaded his weapon, raised himself into a crouched position and aimed directly at the wood panelling underneath the reception deck that Molyneux was using as cover. While his service weapon was not the most powerful, the panelling was undoubtably made of cheap wood and if there was one thing the movies always misjudged, it was just how durable certain types of cover were.

Let's hope, the Deputy thought.

Behind him he could hear approaching sirens.

He held his breath, aimed at where he hoped Karl Molyneux was, and pulled the trigger.

The bullet penetrated the flimsy wood and entered Molyneux's right bicep, hitting the bone and snapping it in two. He dropped his empty pistol as he lost the use of his arm. The pain was incredible. He clutched the entry wound, shut his eyes, and screamed.

This was not supposed to happen. He was meant escape and be long gone from Summerside Lake before the police even knew where he was. It was not his destiny to die here. He was so close!

Not today! Molyneux thought. *NOT TODAY!*

Outside the sirens were deafening. Karl shifted to one of the many holes in the front desk and squinted as he peered through. He could see the Deputy backing away, his gun still drawn, as three separate police cars arrived outside. As the Officers exited their vehicles, some armed with shotguns, two began running to something out of view to Molyneux's left.

"She's with me!" the Deputy shouted. The two Officers hurried her the police line forming in front of the motel. They stood her next to a cruise and joined their colleagues in pointing their service weapons in Molyneux's vicinity.

One of the Officers walked forward with a megaphone.

"Karl Molyneux!" shouted the Officer through the, his voice bouncing off the front façade of the motel. *"We have you surrounded! Come out with your hands raised or we will be forced to open fire! This is your only warning!"*

★

"What are you doing?" Elias shouted at Wiley as the Lieutenant held the megaphone to his face.

"He killed one of ours!" Wiley shouted back, "He's lucky he gets a warning at all!"

Elias saw one of the County Officers putting Annette in handcuffs. He stormed over.

"Hey! Take those off!" he yelled. The Officer stared at the Deputy incredulously.

"She's an escaped convict, sir," he said.

"You take those off right now or I'm writing you up, understand?"

The Officer hesitated before reluctantly nodding and

removing them.

Elias went to Annette and asked, "You ok?"

She nodded.

"Stay down ok?" said Elias as he turned to the officer. "Keep her safe. We don't need another death here tonight."

The Deputy heard the officer sigh and instruct Annette to sit in the back of the nearest cruiser as he walked back toward Wiley.

★

Molyneux did not hesitate. He took one last peek at the congregating wall of armed officers outside before he crouched low and moved as quickly as he could to the proprietor's bedsit. His shoulder briefly appeared above the desk.

It was enough for Wiley.

"*Open fire!*" the Lieutenant screamed, and a fusillade of gun fire erupted. The reception area of Hill Side motel fell apart in pieces as bullets shredded everything they hit. The barrage of noise and destruction lasted less than ten seconds, yet the sheer intensity of the moment felt like a lifetime.

Deputy Ansel ducked behind the nearest squad car as Wiley raised an arm.

"*Cease fire!*" shouted the Lieutenant over the din.

The shooting stopped. Smoke and the smell of cordite lingered in the air as the hollow clatter of spent shotgun shells continued for a few short moments. In the silence Wiley turned and pointed at the two Officers to his left.

"You two, with me," he said and began to walk toward the motel, his gun raised and his trigger finger itchy.

He arrived at the reception flanked by his officers. The room was devastated by the sheer number of rounds fired.

Wiley rounded the desk, gun ready.

Where there should have been a corpse was, instead, wood splinters and fragments of plaster board.

Molyneux was nowhere to be found.

"The fuck?" one of the Officers exclaimed.

There was a trail of blood leading to a door to the right of the reception desk. Wiley sprinted forward and kicked it open.

Inside was the bedsit, which had not escaped gun fire. Beside the bed was the body of Dean Elton, proprietor of the motel, who had clearly suffered a horrific death at the hands of Molyneux.

At the back of the room the curtains billowed in the warm evening air around an open window that exited to the back of the motel. Beyond it was several acres of hop yards. The trail of blood lead into it.

"Fuck!" shouted Wiley before turning to the Officers. "Call it in," he said. "Get Everyone!"

*

"Repeat, Karl Molyneux has escaped. He is armed and extremely dangerous! He has run into the fields behind the Lake

Side motel. Officers are chasing on foot!"

Doug Clark slammed his palm against the steering wheel as he turned his siren on and made a sudden right turn.

There was no need to head to the motel, not anymore. Their fugitive was gone. However, the fields the motel backed onto lead to a place that Doug was very familiar with. It was only a hunch that Molyneux would head there, but it was all the Sheriff had to work with.

As he pushed the gas pedal to the floor, the siren echoing off the passing buildings, he thought about the fastest way to reach the Clark family lumber mill.

THIRTY-ONE

Gillian came to, though her vision was blurred and head pounding. She reached for the bump on her temple before wincing in pain. Looking at her fingers she saw they were drenched in blood. *Heads bleed badly,* she thought to herself in an attempt to stave off panic. *It's not as bad as it looks.*

Their situation, however, was dire.

Trixie was banging against the door to the right of the stage with ever increasing frustration.

"It's fucking *locked!*" she shouted. "Nick?"

"No luck!" came Nick's disembodied voice from the kitchen. "It's padlocked shut!"

"Who the fuck padlocks the service entrance!?" shouted Trixie.

"Someone that doesn't want us to get out," said Gillian quietly. Trixie turned at the sound of her voice and rushed over.

"Shit, you're alive!" Trixie said. *"Nick!"*

Nick came running to see Trixie helping Gillian sit up. He knelt by his injured friend and tried to hug her.

"Hey, easy," Gillian said smiling. "My head hurts like hell."

"I thought you were dead!" said Nick, holding her fiercely. He pulled back and looked at her, concerned.

Gillian gingerly touched the wound on her forehead and asked, "How bad is it?"

"You'll live," said Trixie. "It looks worse than it is." She removed a bandana from her wrist, one of many that helped with the rebel ensemble, and pressed it gently against the wound. Gillian winced and took the sash from Trixie. It was only then she peered to her left and noticed the gruesome spectacle in the centre of the hall.

All color drained from her face.

"Oh my God," she said quietly.

Trixie nodded.

"Who else is hurt?" Gillian asked.

"We don't know," Nick explained solemnly. "Apart from Chad, we've not seen or heard from Conrad, Lucy, or Brandon."

"Did you try the radio?" asked Gillian.

Nick nodded.

"Total bupkis," said Trixie. "And we're stuck in here now it seems."

"The back and side doors are locked," said Nick. "We can try and break open the back door but the amount of noise it'll make will just draw the psycho to us before we can get it open."

"And the side door in the kitchen is padlocked," continued Trixie. "Which means there's only the main door, and he's probably sat out there waiting for us."

"He won't be able to get all of us," said Gillian.

"True, but I'd rather not be the one he *does* get," Trixie said. "Sorry, but I quite like being alive."

Gillian nodded and pulled the sash away from her head. The blood that came away was thick. The wound was plugging up nicely.

She held her hand up to Nick.

"Help me up, would you?" she said.

Both Nick and Trixie helped her to stand. She wobbled as dizziness hit her, though it was less profound than she had feared. She began to walk toward the terrible sight in the middle of the hall, her arm linking with Nick's for stability.

"What were they 'complicit' in?" she asked.

"Hey," said Trixie. Gillian and Nick looked up to see her pointing toward the door to the left of the hall's stage. "What's in there?"

Gillian looked over and said, "That's a storage cupboard. It's just chairs and tables. We checked in there earlier."

"Anything that can help us?" asked Trixie.

"Maybe," said Gillian. "What had you got in mind?"

"Anything that can help us survive," said Trixie.

"I'm pretty sure I saw props in there," said Nick. "You know, things for stage plays. You remember those awful productions they made us do, Trixie?"

Trixie smiled.

"Man, those were bad," she said, chuckling. "I'm gonna have a look."

Nick and Gillian followed Trixie as she walked toward the storage cupboard. Dizziness hit Gillian again and she leaned against Nick for balance.

"I need to sit down," she said.

Nick nodded and helped her sit on the knee-high stage as Trixie open the storage cupboard. He gave Gillian a quick kiss on her cheek before turning to help Trixie.

She leant over a small stack of chairs at the door and slapped the inner walls for a light switch. Nick stood behind her as he heard her squeal "a ha!" and the room illuminated with the stark light of a bare lightbulb.

Along the back wall was an array of items. Among the large pieces of stage scenery were costumes and small props. Trixie's heart sank until she saw, nestled in the furthest corner from the door, a box filled with prop swords. She remembered these; the boys would often hurt each other as they were made of solid wood. Not strong enough to kill but at least it resembled a weapon, and a hard-enough hit to the head could render someone unconscious.

Maybe.

"Great," she said as she leant against a stack of chairs at the door. "Now we've just got to move all this out the way."

Nick peered past her and saw the stacks and stack of chairs

in their way.

"Best get started," he said.

★

"Sheriff? Come in Doug!"

It was Elias.

Doug lifted the radio.

"Everything ok there, son?" the Sheriff asked. He could hear rustling on the other end of the radio.

"Molyneux, he got away."

"I know," said Doug. "I'm on my way to intercept."

There was a beat on the other end of the line.

"Intercept?"

"The lumber yard is directly behind the motel. It's the only thing around for miles."

"He could run straight past it."

"He could, yes, but I'm heading there now," said the Sheriff. "Better to have someone in wait. Just in case."

"And if he avoids it? Decides to take his chances in the woods?"

The Sheriff sighed. They had come so close to capturing their man yet now they were not much closer than they had been that morning.

"Then we cross that bridge when we come to it," he replied. "Listen, I'll be at the lumber yard in minutes. Keep heading in that direction but spread out. And move in pairs. We don't want him getting the drop on a lone cop."

"Roger," said Elias. "I shot him, so be on the lookout for blood."

"Will do," said Doug. "Over and out."

★

Between the two of them, Nick and Trixie removed a sizable amount of furniture in a short time, both aware their assailant could attempt to break the main door down at any minute. Gillian came to help, moving the chairs away from the storeroom door to allow space.

Trixie had passed the next load of chairs to Nick and stepped back into the storeroom when there came a light *crunch* under her foot. She stepped back and peered down to see an old photo in a worn-out frame that was now cracked under her sneaker. Frowning, she knelt, took hold of the photo and as she stood, wiped away some of the grime.

"Hey guys," said Trixie, "come have a look at this."

Nick peered into the storeroom.

"We don't have time for distractions," he said.

Trixie, still looking at the photo, walked over to where Nick stood. Gillian, curious, walked over and joined them.

Inspection showed a faded, posed photograph of eight young camp counselors, all smiling, with a much younger Wallace Asher stood in the middle.

"That's my dad," Trixie said, pointing to a man in the photo that looked startlingly like her.

On the bottom of the frame was an engraving that read:

CAMP SUMMERSIDE COUNSELORS
1959

Trixie squinted and pointed to another young man.

"That's Chad's dad, right there." She trailed her finger across the dusty photo to one of the women. "That's Lucy's mom."

Nick pointed to one of the other men and said, "Shit, that's Rebecca's dad."

"Rebecca?" asked Gillian. "The girl I replaced?"

"Yeah," said Nick distractedly. "Hey, this is everyone's parents. Some of them at least. Well, except mine. From what my Pop told me, he applied for the caretaker job that year but lost it to Stephen Haig."

Trixie wiped more grime off the picture and pointed to a young woman stood to the edge of the photograph.

"I don't know who that is," she said.

Gillian did. It took a moment, but the round, innocent face was familiar, one she had seen only a few hours before with the added mask of age, but she recognised her all the same.

"Wait, is that-" began Nick.

"Yes, it is," Gillian interrupted. At the bottom of the picture were the names of those in it. Though she never introduced herself, Gillian now had a name to match the face.

Annette Maxwell.

There was a sudden banging at the main door that made the trio jump. It was the forceful, repetitive thumping of someone panicked.

"Jesus! Let me in!"

It was Marco.

★

Sheriff Clark turned left onto a dirt track and past an imposing green sign with the Clark Lumber Yard company logo embossed on it. Since Doug had left the company to pursue his career in law enforcement, the running of the yard had fallen to his brother, Jim after their father had retired.

The gates were locked yet the Sheriff did not slow.

"Sorry Jim," he muttered to himself as he drove into the gate, sheering the padlock and bending the frame. He sped along the entry road and into the main parking lot with more commotion that he would have liked but time was crucial.

The Sheriff came to a stop in the parking lot, which was next to the 'temporary' office structure that had been there for close to twenty years. He waited a few moments: there were no lights on in the office and he saw and heard no signs of human activity.

Molyneaux, it seemed, had not yet arrived.

The Sheriff gingerly parked the car behind the office and turned off the head lights. It would not do to have Molyneux see Doug's cruiser waiting for him.

Clark shut down the engine and exited the vehicle. He

opened the trunk and pulled back a musty, beige blanket to reveal a pump action twelve-gauge shotgun. He lifted it and loaded six rounds from the open box of ammunition stored next to it.

As he pumped the shotgun and closed the trunk, Doug heard a hurried rustling approaching from opposite the office. Doug peered around the building to see the wall of hops that bordered the yard about one-hundred metres opposite him.

The rustling grew louder.

A shape emerged from the foliage, the stalks towering above them. Its arm was dangling limply to its side.

I shot him, so be on the lookout for blood.

The shape stared around the yard at a loss. There was shouting behind him from his pursuers.

Doug had to smile. There was a grim satisfaction in seeing the monster a step behind the law for once.

Molyneux stared at the office and sprinted toward it.

The Sheriff would wait. It was refreshing to have the criminal come to him.

THIRTY-TWO

"**F**uck," said Trixie as Marco continued to hammer on the door. Nick began to walk forward when she placed a hand on his arm.

"What are you doing?" she asked.

"We can't leave him out there," said Nick.

"After what I did to him?" she said. "If we let him in, he'll just try and finish what he started!"

"I'm amazed he can walk," said Gillian wryly.

"So, we make sure he *doesn't* finish what he started," said Nick. "There's three of us. What can he do?"

Trixie folded her arms.

"You'd be surprised," she said.

"Look, I can't leave him out there in good conscience with a madman out there," Nick protested.

"Christ! Let me *in* guys!" Marco screamed. "I found Lucy and Chad! They're dead! Please don't leave me out here!"

"Listen," said Nick to Trixie, "you can lean across and grab what you need from the storeroom now. Let me go to the door and you can get something to defend yourself with, ok?"

Behind them came a clatter. Trixie and Nick turned toward the storeroom to see Gillian clambering over the remaining furniture and out of view.

"Gill!" Nick yelled. "Be careful!"

A sturdy piece of wood in the basic shape of a sword flew through the doorway of the storeroom and rattled on the floor. Another followed a second later.

"Guys! *PLEASE!*" screamed Marco.

Gillian emerged from the storeroom with a third weapon, collected the other two, and approached Nick and Trixie. She handed them a prop each.

"Better safe than sorry," she said.

Nick nodded as Trixie approached the door.

"Marco?" she called.

"Oh, thank *god!*" he shouted. "What the fuck are you doing in there? Let me in!"

"You gonna play nice?" asked Trixie.

"Are you fucking high!?" Marco yelled. "There's a killer out here and you're worried about me?! *JUST LET ME IN!*"

Trixie looked at her companions. Gillian raised her weapon above her head and nodded. Nick followed suit.

Trixie rested her hand on the lock and said, "I'm opening the door now. Stand back ok?"

"Thank fucking Christ!" Marco shouted in return.

Trixie clicked the lock, grabbed the door handle, and opened the door.

Marco grinned as he pointed a bright orange flare gun directly at her face.

"Surprise, bitch," he said.

★

Karl Molyneux made it to the office at a sprint and Doug Clark listened as the fugitive tentatively tried the door handle. When it did not open he took a step back and kicked the flimsy thing off its hinges. Molyneux bolted inside and began rummaging through the drawers of the nearest desk to the door. Doug was familiar with the layout of the office and knew there were three desks and four relatively large filing cabinets. What Molyneux expected to find was any guess to Doug, but it was a distraction he could exploit.

The Sheriff came out from hiding and began to silently ascend the stairs to the open office door.

★

The flare gun was a great find.

When Marco stumbled to the green with aching, swollen testicles he headed straight to the medical hut. There had to be some painkillers in there.

He barely gave Chad's dismembered body a second glance.

SUMMERSIDE LAKE MASSACRE

Got what you deserved Pretty Boy.

As he stumbled into the hut he spied the flare gun out the corner of his eye next to the destroyed radio. He picked it up and as he checked it was loaded – it was – he spotted Lucy's corpse. Along with the bloodied foot in the green outside, it became obvious that some serious shit was taking place at Camp Summerside since he had left.

Well, Marco thought, *better them than me.*

That was when he heard the sound of Trixie's voice coming from the windows of the main hall and a delicious plan came to be.

*

The gun was raised at the one person he had hoped would open the door, though he was happy to fire the flare in the face of whoever answered. His idea was for the flare to kill the person behind the door and ignite the main hall, burning it and whoever was in it to the ground. But upon seeing Trixie's face he could not help but smile.

"Surprise, bitch," he said.

The axe soared down on his extended arm and severed his hand just below the wrist. His hand fell to the ground clutching the flare gun with a dull thud. Marco pulled his arm back and raised the bloody stump to his face. Realisation and pain hit him like a one-two punch and he screamed harder than he ever had in his life.

★

Karl looked up from the desk he had been rummaging through as the light in the doorway dimmed. The figure stood with a shotgun pointed at him.

"Don't move," he said calmly in the silence.

Karl sighed.

"You guys don't quit, do you?" he said.

"Raise your hands and walk towards me," said the Sheriff.

"You said don't move," Molyneux said smirking.

"I wouldn't test me if I were you," said Clark. "It doesn't faze me one way another if you're alive when back-up arrives."

Karl's smile faltered.

"I didn't realise this was the wild west," he said.

"It was the wild west the moment you killed my Deputies."

Karl's smile returned.

"Ah, you must be our good Sheriff," he said. "I don't believe we've been formally acquainted."

"Karl Molyneux, I'm arresting you for the murders of Deputies Alan Pratchett and Thomas Foster, Officer Ronald Jackson, and Dean Elton. You have the right to remain silent. Anything you say can and will be used-"

Molyneux flipped the desk, despite his injury. Clark fired the shotgun, the round scattering and hitting Molyneux in the shoulder and cheek. He let out a scream as the impact sent him backward. The Sheriff walked forward and pumped the shotgun, the shell casing flying from the weapon and clattering on the office floor. The fugitive looked up at him in shock as Clark approached, the shotgun's barrel levelled at his face.

"Stop resisting Karl," he said calmly.

Outside, sirens approached.

Molyneux tried to push himself up.

"I said, stop resisting," the Sheriff repeated.

Karl looked from the weapon to the man wielding it.

"It's illegal to gun down an unarmed man," he said.

The Sheriff nodded.

"But not a fleeing one," said Doug as he aimed down the sights.

The color drained from Karl's face. Doug finally saw fear in the killer's eyes.

"*Gun, gun, gun!*" came a shout from behind the Sheriff. Before he could react, a small bloody hole appeared on Karl Molyneux's temple a fraction before the back of his head blew outwards. The contents of his skull splattered the window behind him as his body slumped.

Doug spun around to see Deputy Ansel stood close behind him, pistol drawn.

*

Marco had barely noticed the killer to his right, he was so focused on the injury he had sustained. He looked up to see the axe that had just removed his hand fly toward his face where it connected with a wet *crack* as it embedded itself in his jaw. The force sent him on his backside. He heard his mandible shatter and dislodge as he fell. By the time he hit the ground his entire lower jaw was a bloody, bony mess, hanging useless from his face.

As the killer stood and watched Marco flail and shout a gargled, disbelieving scream, he heard a cry from behind him. He turned in time to see the nerdy kid running toward him with what appeared to be a wooden sword.

The killer stepped to one side as Nick brought his weapon down. The action sent the kid off balance and the killer took the opportunity to hit him across the face. Nick was unconscious before he hit the ground. The killer stared at his prone form inquisitively before Marco's cries earned his attention.

Marco was a mess. He was crawling away from the main hall, weeping uncontrollably and leaving a trail of blood with him. How he had not passed out, the killer did not know, but it was time to finish the job.

Behind him he could hear the ginger girl shouting for Nick to get up.

The killer reached Marco and kicked him onto his back. Before the kid could react, the killer leant down and took hold of the ruined mandible like one would a handle and lifted. The scream from Marco was loud and excruciating as he frantically attempted to bat away the killer's hand.

"I told you I'd make you smile," the killer said as he removed the hunting knife he had used to murder Chad from its sheath and rammed it into the side of Marco's head with enough force to pierce the skull and enter his brain. His victim's eyes fluttered and his muscles spasmed, his hand clenching around the killer's mask. As the killer dropped Marco, the corpse's vice like grip tore the mask away from the killer's face.

The killer felt a sudden, blunt pain in his side accompanied by a scream of defiance. Trixie brought her wooden sword back up for another attack when the killer turned and caught the weapon before impact.

He stared at her with unparalleled fury.

For the briefest of moments, Trixie was struck dumb as she looked at the killer's unmasked face.

Her assailant held the carving knife above his head to strike.

"Hold it!" screamed Gillian.

Both Trixie and the killer turned to see Gillian pointing the flare gun at them.

*

As more police cruisers arrived at the scene of Karl Molyneux's last stand, Deputy Ansel walked into the office and removed a second pistol from his belt.

The Sheriff did not stop him.

Elias walked past Doug and said, "His weapon. From the motel."

The Deputy calmly placed the gun in Molyneux's hand and closed the fugitive's fingers around the grip.

*

It was Gillian's turn to go dumb as the killer faced her and Nick.

"Put that down girl," said Conrad Ellis, calmly. "You could hit Trixie."

"Just shoot him!" Trixie yelled.

"You!" was all Gillian could manage.

Conrad brought the knife down onto Trixie's shoulder, where the blade bounced off the bone and carved an enormous wound down her shoulder blade. Trixie screamed and recoiled, letting go of her weapon before attempting to bat away Conrad's now free hand as it took her by the hair. He pulled the counselor against him and put the knife to her throat.

He smiled at Gillian and said, "How about now?"

Gillian froze.

"Go on, shoot me!" the killer screamed.

Gillian's arms tremored as she pointed the flare gun at them. Trixie stared at her, eyes ablaze with fear.

"C'mon!" Conrad goaded.

Trixie stared at the flare gun then back at Gillian. Something passed between them, an understanding of what must be done.

Gillian began to weep.

"I'm sorry," she said.

Trixie simply nodded.

"Do it!" Conrad cried.

"Fuck you!" Gillian screamed at as she raised the flare gun above her head and fired it into the night sky.

THIRTY-THREE

Doug and Elias were exiting the office of Clark Lumber Yard when the sky across the lake illuminated with a bright red fire. All the officers in the parking lot turned and raised their hands against the light.

"What the hell?" asked Elias.

The Sheriff knew, though he had never seen the flare be used. He turned and sprinted to his cruiser.

"Doug?" Elias called after him.

"Emergency flare!" Doug shouted back. "From Camp Summerside!"

He opened the driver's side door, slammed it shut, and turned on the ignition. He sped out of the parking lot with his red and blues flashing.

★

The flare hovered over Camp Summerside for what seemed like an eternity. From above, the camp and its surrounding woodland basked in a concentrated red brightness, arching upward from where it had been fired, before it sputtered and petered out, sending the camp back into darkness.

In the square, Conrad stared back at Gillian. They locked eyes; the counselor's defiant, the killer's raging.

"They won't arrive in time," Conrad said and slit Trixie's throat.

Gillian screamed in anguish as her friend fell to her knees, clutching her neck. Trixie reached a bloody hand forward in a vain attempt for help before keeling forward.

Conrad ignored her and stepped over her dying body toward Gillian.

Gillian squatted and grabbed the wooden sword at her feet as Conrad reached forward and grabbed her by the hair. The counselor yelled in pain and weakly hit her attacker in the side with the sword, an act Conrad was able to deflect with little effort.

"Stop it!" he screamed with enough rage and volume to cull Gillian into shock.

"Why?" she asked, her eyes ablaze.

"Not you or Nick," Conrad said with a trace of remorse. "The others, yes, but not you. You weren't even meant to be here. It should be Rebecca on the other end of this knife. But I can't let you live. You've seen too much."

Gillian glanced at the knife twitching in his hand.

SUMMERSIDE LAKE MASSACRE

"For what it's worth, I'm sorry," he said.

Conrad pulled the knife back, the tip aimed at her abdomen.

At his feet, there was a *snap* not unlike a twig. He peered down to see Nick brandishing a thin but pointed piece of metal, his glasses resting broken beside him.

Nick stabbed the arm of his glasses with force at the soft flesh between Conrad's ankle and Achilles tendon. The killer screamed and let go of Gillian's hair, raising the knife above his head and slashing down. The blade hit Nick just below his right eye and cut down to his cheek bone, continuing down and slicing through his nose. Nick screamed as the tip of his nose was reduced to no more than a skin flap that dangled from his face. He relinquished his hold on his makeshift weapon and clutched his wounds with both hands as he wailed in pain.

Gillian came at Conrad with her wooden sword, filled with rage, and struck him in the side of his knee. The impact sent him off balance, pitching him in the opposite direction from where he had been hit. The full weight of his body buckled on his now damaged knee and as he toppled, he felt bones, cartilage, and tendons begin to break and snap as his knee bent sideways.

Before gravity took full hold, he clutched Gillian by the neck. They fell to the ground together.

*

Elias radioed the Sheriff advising he wait for back up, yet Doug declined. With much of the police force now at the scene of

Molyneux's death, there would be few officers close enough to help.

Doug clicked off and called for both an ambulance and a fire truck to meet him at Camp Summerside as soon as possible.

There was no way of knowing what would await him when he arrived.

The Sheriff hit the gas and left the siren blaring.

★

Gillian's head hit the dirt with enough force for her to see stars for a second time. There was an audible snap as her weight broke the wooden sword in two. As she lay there, she felt a blistering pain erupt from her abdomen.

Opposite her on the ground was Conrad. He was grinning.

Gillian looked down to see the hunting knife in her stomach.

Conrad pulled the knife from her and she bowed forward in pain and shock. Her attacker assessed his mangled knee and the piece of metal sticking from his ankle. He pinched the arm from Nick's glasses and began to pull. The sensation stung like nothing he had ever felt and as it was pulled from his flesh, he let out a growl through clenched teeth.

He gasped as it finally came free and threw it petulantly at Nick, who was still holding his face. His would-be assailant had not broken the tendon.

He began the laborious task of standing on his good leg as the last two counselors writhed around him. It was regrettable that they would have to die, yet they had not gone down without a fight, which he admired. Conrad had not, however, expected his counselors to be so dammed tenacious.

Once everything was done, he would need to disappear of course. At his apartment was a small bag that included a change of clothes, fake ID, and three-hundred dollars in cash. It was enough to get him to the east coast. From there he had no idea where he would go. He had also prepared a care package for the police. They would inevitably look to him as a suspect when his body was not found among the dead, and in that package was a letter explaining his reasons, planning, and evidence to support many of the claims within.

It was signed: *From Waldo.*

Right now, however, there was a job to finish.

He noticed the sound of an approaching siren. Just the one. It was getting closer, its wail echoing through the night air.

It was never part of Conrad's plan to kill a cop, but if it was needed in order to facilitate his escape, it would be yet another regrettable but necessary death.

Conrad hobbled past Nick toward the fire axe that lay discarded outside the main hall. Sure, his knife would be more than adequate to kill them, but an axe was quicker. No need to prolong their demise any further.

He squatted with difficulty and grabbed the axe by the handle. As he stood, he winced and sighed.

"Let's get this over with," he said and pivoted on his one good leg to face his final two victims.

Conrad's heart skipped a beat and, as the first very real twinges of fear hit him, he nearly dropped the axe.

Gillian was gone.

★

As Doug skidded left at the junction connecting the main road to the long dirt track that eventually led to Camp Summerside, he was informed over the radio that the ambulance and fire department would arrive roughly five minutes after him.

He prayed that they would not be too late.

★

"GILLIAN!" Conrad screamed into the clearing as the sound of sirens grew closer. *"You don't understand! This has to be done!"*

There was no reply.

Conrad stared around the clearing. Everything beyond it was pitch dark and where he was stood, between the medical hut and the main hall, bordered where the light ended, and night began.

He turned and looked into the darkness behind him.

"You have ten seconds to show yourself!" he shouted. "Ten seconds! After that I kill your boyfriend!"

There was no reply.

"One!"

Still nothing.

Conrad turned to Nick who was staring back at him, his face

a mess of blood and flayed skin.

The killer took a step toward him.

"Two!"

★

Gillian hid behind the nearest tree, clutching the wound at her side while brandishing what was left of the broken sword.

"*Three!*"

She had gritted through her own pain and scurried into the darkness while his back was turned, collecting his weapon. It was when he moved to investigate the shadows behind him that she froze, holding her breath and hoping, just hoping, that his eyes would not adjust.

"*Four!*"

As she peered around the tree, their eyes had met and held for what seemed like a lifetime. *He's seen me,* she thought, *of course he's seen me.* How could he have not when she was not even ten meters from him? There was nothing obscuring his view of her face.

Why didn't I just run? she thought.

Because Nick needed saving.

Conrad turned to Nick then and made his threat.

He hasn't seen me! Gillian thought.

"*Five!*"

"Don't do it Gill!" shouted Nick. "Get out of here!"

"*Six!*"

Gillian's resolve hardened. Her knuckles were white around the broken piece of wood she held.

The *pointed* broken piece of wood.

She knew what she had to do.

She stepped out from behind the tree and into the light, where Conrad and fate waited.

★

Nick's gaze shifted from Conrad to something behind him. It was slight but it was enough.

Conrad rounded to see Gillian brandishing what looked like a stake over her head. Before he could bring the fire axe up to defend himself, Gillian brought the broken piece of wood down with all her remaining strength. It connected with the soft tissue between his collar bone and the base of his neck, penetrating the skin before splinters caught on flesh and tendons.

Conrad gasped and his eyes widened. He batted away Gillian's extended arm and hit her square in the face with the shaft of the axe. The girl fell to the ground, blood streaming from her nose as she landed on her back, her legs splayed. She stared up to see Conrad lifting the axe over his head. His silhouette was a peculiar mix of horror and absurdity, his threatening pose scuppered by the chunk of wood sticking comically from his neck.

His face was a mask of abject rage.

So, this will be my end? Gillian thought. *Like* this?!

SUMMERSIDE LAKE MASSACRE

Then she heard the gun shot.

★

The Sheriff had turned off the siren as he rounded the corner to see the archway for Camp Summerside coming toward him out of the darkness. Apart from the lights in the central green, the rest of the camp was dark save for flashes of red and blue from his cruiser.

Doug shut down the engine and leaped from the car, his shotgun already against his shoulder. With the events of the evening so far, he would not take any chances.

"*Six!*" came a deep scream.

Doug sprinted and took cover against the wall of the medical hut and gingerly peered around its corner.

The scene was not what he expected.

In the green's centre was a severed foot still in its shoe, which was surrounded by a brown pool of coagulated blood. To his right, one of the doors to the main hall was wide open. Not far from it were three figures that Doug recognised from earlier.

The punk girl was dead her neck a mess of fresh blood and ragged flesh while her eyes were wide and saw nothing.

Stood over one of the other counselors, the young black kid, was Conrad Ellis, covered from head to toe in blood. In his hands was a large fire axe.

The Sheriff watched as the girl with fiery red hair stepped out from the darkness, herself dishevelled and wounded, as she raised a weapon over her head to strike. He watched the bizarre scene unfold, as she stabbed her boss, as Conrad beat her with the fire axe, and as he stood over her, gravely wounded, ready to kill as the injured kid screamed for him not to.

Doug gave no warning. He brought his weapon to his shoulder, aimed, and fired.

★

The back of Conrad's head exploded in a halo of red meat, bone, and brain matter. There was the briefest register of confusion on his face, as if wondering if he had left the stove on, before parts of the inside of his head exited through his nose and mouth, and his eyes bulged unnaturally. The force of the blast threw his body forward as if being hit with a blunt object, sending his now lifeless body stumbling to its knees where it hung for a second before toppling onto its front.

The sudden silence was deafening. Gillian stared transfixed at the corpse before her, the mortal wound glistening in the oscillating glow of the cruiser's lights.

"Gillian?"

She came out of her trance at the sound of Nick's voice and saw him staring at her. His face, his lovable, goofy face, was a mess.

But he was alive.

She did not notice the pain in her abdomen as she crawled over to him. She turned him on his back and rested his head in her lap where she ran stroked his head and comforted him. They sat like that for what seemed like forever before they noticed the sound of approaching footsteps.

The Sheriff knelt in front of them with two blankets and a first aid kit. He lay one blanket over Nick and one around Gillian's shoulders.

"There's help on the way," said Doug as he unpackaged a fresh sterile pad and placed it gently on Nick's face. The boy winced. "You'll be ok, I promise."

Gillian nodded. Her eyes stared off into the distance, not looking, just glazed, the cruiser's red and blue lights dancing off her face. It was a stare Doug had never personally seen but knew of. It was reserved for those in extreme shock.

The Sheriff looked around the green until his gaze turned to the medical hut, where young Chad Edwards rested, his hand at the terrible wound in his gut and his eyes as lifeless as Trixie's.

What the hell happened here? he thought.

From a distance, additional sirens could be heard. The ambulance, most likely, or the fire engine, and judging by the carnage he was seeing they would need a lot more than that.

Doug waited with the counselors, the only survivors of a terrible ordeal, as the sirens grew louder.

TWO WEEKS LATER

"We all go a little mad sometimes."

Psycho, 1960

Nick smiled when he heard the knock at the door. Although the smile caused tremendous pain, as the swelling was still prominent, his facial wound still healing, he was happy all the same.

The doctors had been honest with him; the scar would be significant, and they could not guarantee his nose could be saved. They had tried as best they could. Ligaments and muscles had been painstakingly reconstructed in his cheek as well as the attempted reattachment of his nose, but he and the doctors were under no illusions that his face would be obviously different for the rest of his life.

He was afraid of being discharged.

Both Nick and Gillian had been in the hospital since their ordeal. Though police had concluded that Conrad had worked alone, that did not stop the nightmares. They came every night, each more vivid than the last, to the point where Nick had woken one night screaming with such terror that he had to be sedated. Despite the dreams, he felt safe where he was. There was a police guard stationed at his door to ward off any journalists, conspiracy theorists, or the morbidly curious. This protection would cease once he was sent home.

But that was not the only reason.

He was now scarred, and badly. His wound would draw attention he did not want. People could be cruel, but he did not want their sympathy either. He had survived where his friends had not, and his face would be a daily reminder of that fact.

However, for now, his mood was elevated by his guest.

The door opened and Gillian was brought in on a wheelchair that was pushed by a friendly orderly. Nick had no idea of the woman's name, but she was kind and had updated him on his friend's process.

Gillian's injury was worse than initially feared. The knife had penetrated nearly to her spine and caused significant damage to her liver and small intestines. Once surgeons had stopped the bleeding, she was moved to a room of her own and pumped with enough antibiotics to raise the dead. And now, though she was on the mend, her body was still weak.

The next few months would be a rough road, but they would be ok.

"Hey!" said Nick happily.

Gillian smiled. She was gaunt but in good spirits.

"Hey yourself," she said in that self-assured way that Nick

had come to love so much.

The orderly wheeled Gillian over to Nick's bedside and rested a hand on her shoulder.

"I'll be back in an hour. If you need anything, just call the guard outside."

Gillian patted the orderly's hand and said a quite thank you before the lady left them alone.

"So, going for the Boris Karloff look I see," said Gillian.

Nick laughed and winced. The bandages still covered much of his head.

"Yeah, I think it looks good on me," he said. "It comes off today though."

"So, I heard," Gillian said.

Nick reached forward and took her hand. They linked fingers and held each other tenderly.

"How are you doing?" Nick asked.

"Better I guess," said Gillian, her smile faltering. "The doctors say it'll be a long road before I'm back on my feet."

Nick could only nod.

"I still see him you know," Gillian continued.

"Every night?"

"Every night. Sometimes when I wake up, I get confused and forget where I am. I swear he's stood there watching me when I sleep. I know he's not, but still."

"Same," said Nick.

They sat in silence. The bustle of the hospital outside the room was muted as they held hands. For better or worse, they were now forever joined in both survival and trauma.

"Why do you think he did it?" Nick asked, not for the first time.

Gillian shrugged.

"I'm sure we'll eventually find out," she said. "I've been told that Sheriff Clark wants to talk to us again as soon as we're able."

"Great," Nick sighed. "I'd sooner forget it all, if it's all the same to him."

"I'm sure it's just a formality," said Gillian.

"What else does he need to know?"

Gillian shrugged and said, "Our version of events, I guess, now we're not on death's door." She held his hand tighter. "I hear you'll be discharged tomorrow?"

Nick tried to smile.

"Word gets around," he said. "But yes, if the wound still looks like its improving, I should be out of here by tomorrow. The day after at the latest."

"That's great," Gillian said with genuine warmth. "I'll be here for a while longer, I think. Turns out having your guts cut open is great for getting sepsis."

"How long do you think?"

"Another month. I should be off the antibiotics soon but need to get my strength up again." She smiled again. "I never thought I'd be in rehab at seventeen but there we go."

"Not that kind of rehab," said Nick seriously.

Gillian rolled her eyes.

"I know *that*," she said. "Jeeze! My humor is wasted on you."

Nick laughed again. It was good to see flickers of his friend return, however briefly. It would take time, and there would be days where neither of them would want to face the world, but humor was always a good sign.

"Gillian?" he asked.

She turned and looked at him expectantly.

"I'm glad I met you," he said.

Gillian lifted their conjoined hands and gently kissed his.

"Me too," she said with a smile.

★

Sheriff Clark looked up from his desk to find Deputy Ansel at his door. Doug waved him in and leaned back in his chair. Elias appeared upbeat as he sat opposite his boss.

"A bit of light reading there I see?" asked the Deputy, nodding to the pile of paperwork before Doug.

"Our man *really* wanted to see this town crumble," said Doug as he reached forward, collected a small, stapled pile of paper, and handed it to Elias. "Have a look at this."

The Deputy took it and stared at the photocopied pages.

"What's this?" he asked.

"It was found at Wallace Asher's residence along with his body. It would appear Wallace was fond of jotting down his every thought. I knew the man liked the sound of his own voice, but these pages paint himself as a misunderstood genius."

"Christ," said Elias. "and how much was there?"

"Half a room," said Doug. "One side of his study was filled with shelves of leather-bound ledgers, all filled by him."

"Seems excessive."

"Yes, but it's a goldmine for us," said Doug, pointing to the photocopies in Elias's hand. "Read page three."

Elias did as the Sheriff put his feet upon his desk and sipped his coffee. The Deputy's brow grow progressively creased.

"So," Elias eventually said, still staring at the page, "Conrad was correct."

Doug nodded.

"It would appear so," he said.

★

The police had raided the home of Conrad Ellis only hours after his killing spree at Camp Summerside. What they found startled them.

His residence was a mess, totally at odds with his public persona. On the main wall of the living room was a series of printouts and handwritten notes about various people from Summerside Hills, all of whom were either working at Camp Summerside during its inaugural summer or were active and prominent town figures back in nineteen fifty-nine. These included the likes of Wallace Asher, Stephen Haig, Judge Atwell, and the warden of Lake Side hospital, Brett Martin. There was a big red cross over Brett's name, presumably due to his death from cancer in the late seventies. The rest appeared to be fair game.

What startled investigators the most, however, were the photos and notes made on the children of the original nineteen fifty-nine counselors. They were extensive enough to fill enough notebooks to make Wallace Asher jealous.

★

"I'm guessing he was our fabled Man in Black that Annette Maxwell kept speaking of?" asked Elias.

"He was," said Doug. Conrad had admitted as much in his letter to the police.

"But why did he do that?" asked the Deputy. "That's the part I still don't get. Why was Karl Molyneux important enough to help his escape?"

"Molyneux meant nothing to him," said Doug. "He was a means to an end, nothing more."

"To *what* end though?"

"A distraction," said Doug. "He was a dangerous enough criminal to warrant attention from all sides of the law. So many resources would be dedicated to re-capturing him that there would be little to none left should assistance be needed at Camp Summerside. He made damn sure no help was coming."

"Then why blackmail Judge Atwell? If Conrad was planning on causing a scene at Lake Side, why all the preamble to blackmail Atwell into getting Molyneux moved?"

Doug shrugged.

"He didn't say. I'm guessing it was a power play. To show the Judge that he wasn't the only one who could bend the law when it suited him."

Elias nodded. What the Judge had done to ensure Annette Maxwell's incarceration was appalling.

"Then why not kill him?" the Deputy asked. "Why not take out Atwell like he did the others?"

"I think he would've done, had I not shot him," said Doug.

★

There was much that Conrad had not mentioned in his letter but his confession to the police was thorough enough for them to be able to determine his motives.

Conrad Ellis spent much of his childhood in foster care and adapted to the often harsh conditions quickly. Any form of weakness was exploited by those that meant harm, so he developed a tough façade early. It was a trait he developed over time and utilised in his adult life to help become a successful businessman in New York.

He only became curious of his birth parents in his late twenties - through his own investigations into their whereabouts, Conrad was able to find records that showed his mother was still alive, yet his father was never documented. His mother's last known address had been a suburb of a small town in the Pacific Northwest called Summerside Hills, yet upon visiting the location, he was met with a wall of silence as to his mother's most recent residence.

It was as he delved into the town's archives that he found that his mother was still alive, though she had been a resident at Lake Side hospital for the Criminally Insane since the early sixties. The certificate determining her mental viability, or lack thereof, was signed by non-other than Judge Atwell and Brett Martin.

The patient's name was Annette Maxwell.

*

"Where is she now?" asked Elias.

"She's back at Lake Side for the time being, though considering her circumstances, her time there will be coming to an end. She'll need therapy but the state seems happy to supply this to her." Doug suddenly appeared grave. "I doubt she'll be able to fully trust anyone ever again."

*

That was not all Conrad found during his diggings.

Prior to her incarceration, his birth mother had worked a summer at the recently opened Camp Summerside across the lake, yet any record of what had happened in the time between her working there and her internment, which was only two months, had disappeared. This was strange in as much as there would usually be some kind of records, medical or otherwise, that say what had led Annette Maxwell to lose all her mental capacities at such a young age.

There was little for Conrad to work with other than a photograph of his mother that was taken on the day Camp Summerside opened. In it were her fellow counselors and the founder of the camp, Wallace Asher. Conrad checked names against addresses and was surprised to find that, apart from his mother, the original counselors as well as Wallace Asher all still resided in Summerside Hills.

He struck gold with David Edwards.

The editor and chief of the Summerside Gazette was known for frequenting the local dive also visited by the town's lawmakers, and it was on Conrad's second visit to the venue that he first approached Edwards with a drink and a smile.

★

"Edwards?" said Doug. "We've got a couple of Wiley's men heading over to his home this morning. I'll tell you, I really wanted to be the guy to put the handcuffs on him, but we'll let Wiley have this one. Bit of a gut punch really: being told your son has been killed only to be arrested hours later."

"What about the others?" asked Elias.

"The others?"

"The other parents. The ones of the victims."

"Edwards is the first," said Doug. "Wiley and his men will be bringing in the other parents through the day."

★

SUMMERSIDE LAKE MASSACRE

It turned out that Edwards, once drunk, had a tendency to dwell on the sins of his past.

Conrad remained cool as he offered to walk the man home, but David Edwards was speaking of things that made his blood boil. There was regret in his tone, but that did not excuse the fact that, during Camp Summerside's inaugural summer, he had participated is a truly wretched crime. And if Edwards to be believed he was not alone. The other male counselors were equally guilty and the female members by proxy due to their silence. Even the damned caretaker, Stephen Haig, failed to intervene.

And what of Asher? His involvement was the most grievous, for it was he that initiated the first mechanisms that led to Annette's eventual declaration of insanity.

Once he had seen Edwards home there was the beginnings of something forming in his brain. Yet he needed confirmation, not just the ramblings of a drunk, pathetic man.

Conrad headed to the hospital.

It was surprising how easily he was able to stroll around with purpose and not be questioned. Maybe it was the suit he wore or the sheer confidence he emanated, yet he was able to access archives with little to no problems. It took time and the files were well hidden, but he eventually found the paperwork for Annette Maxwell's admittance to Lake Side hospital.

It was a distressing read, yet it confirmed in full what Edwards had told him.

The doctor's notes determined that, on examination of the

patient, there were significant injuries associated with aggressive and likely non-consensual intercourse. Swabs also showed samples of sperm from at least five different men.

★

Elias ran his fingers through his hair and sighed.

"What's eating you Deputy?" asked the Sheriff.

"Ok, I'm just going to ramble here as I'm still trying to get my head around all this but correct me if I'm wrong, ok?"

"Ok."

"Conrad finds out his biological mother is Annette Maxwell, and that she's been declared insane. But he's sceptical as to why she's gone from sane to *in*sane in the space of two months."

"Correct."

"So, in his digging he finds out she was one of the counselors during Camp Summerside's first summer. He also finds out through David Edwards that the male counselors, including Edwards himself, assaulted her. Yet rather than them facing the consequences, Asher, worried on how this would look on his new business venture, conspired to ensure Maxwell remained quiet."

"Also correct."

★

Getting Wallace Asher to sell the camp was easy.

SUMMERSIDE LAKE MASSACRE

The proprietor was standing on a pile of debt that he could barely keep track of, the pressure of which had led him to drink heavily. He did not question Conrad's motives. He took the young man's story of the stresses of big city living at face value. And why not, when a massive cheque was being thrust in your face? What Ellis was offering would more than pay for the camp itself as well as clear his outstanding debts.

And the stain of that first summer would finally be clean.

Once he signed the deeds over, it was as if a great weight had been lifted. This burden was no longer his.

It would only be three weeks later that this young man would murder him in his own home.

*

"So where did Judge Atwell come into this?" Elias asked.

"You forget," said Doug, "the original counselors were the children of very influential people in town. If news got out that some or all their kids had been involved in such a crime, their status, their businesses, everything about them would have crumbled. It was in their interest to ensure Maxwell didn't talk. And it was in Atwell's interest to keep such powerful constituents happy."

"So, he declared her insane," said Elias.

"He did," said Doug. "But the night Annette was admitted to hospital for her assault was when Karl Molyneux committed his killing spree. That was a much bigger deal than one teenager's cry of rape and it was exploited as such."

Elias leaned back in his seat and exhaled heavily.

"Jesus Christ," he said.

The Sheriff could only nod.

"What about her parents?" the Deputy continued.

"What about them? They had members of authority telling them that their daughter had a complete mental breakdown. This was the fifties, remember? You trusted what the police and government told you. Plus, they were older parents. They were both in their forties when Annette was born, and they just accepted their daughter was sick as well the recommendations of the town's psychiatrist. It must have been devastating for them. And the more Annette tried to convince others she wasn't crazy, the less authentic she appeared. It was a vicious cycle."

"For twenty-five years though," said Elias. "No wonder she's a mess."

Doug nodded and said, "We'll ensure she gets the help she needs. And with Asher's journals, we may be able to formulate a prosecution, but I can't guarantee it. The hospital would have taken swabs when Annette was admitted but it's entirely possible that evidence has disappeared. Without it, it'll be a struggle.

"I feel sorry for Conrad, in a weird way."

Elias raised an eyebrow.

"You do?" he said.

"I do. Imagine finding out that not only was your birth mother treated that way but that you're also a child of rape. It'd be a lot for anyone to take in."

SUMMERSIDE LAKE MASSACRE

"Why the kids though?" asked Elias. "All the people from fifty-nine are still here in town so why not go after them directly? He killed Wallace and Haig."

"Because Wallace and Haig didn't have children," said the Sheriff. "Did you read Conrad's confession?"

"Not all of it," admitted Elias. "Too much righteous anger."

"He went for their children because they were innocent. He wanted to take their innocence in the same way their parents took away his mother's."

Elias nodded. There were many variables that could have completely ruined Conrad's plan but if digging further into his history revealed anything it was that he had a penchant for the theatrical. Any one of the victims could have refused their job offers and, as with Rebecca, some could have simply not arrived for induction day.

"How are the survivors?" Elias asked.

"They're good considering," Doug said. "They were only connected by proxy. But we'll help them too."

Silence fell between them. It was a mess the likes of which Sheriff Clark had never seen. He was already fending off calls for interviews.

Much like the Molyneux spree twenty-five years earlier, the murders at Camp Summerside would forever be a stain on the legacy of the town.

On his desk among the piles of paperwork was that morning's edition of USA Today. The headline read:

SUMMERSIDE LAKE MASSACRE!
WHAT DO WE KNOW ABOUT DERANGED KILLER?

No-one cares about the victims, Doug thought bitterly.

EPILOGUE

"**G**ill? You awake?"

Gillian turned in her bed to see Nick laying there. Despite the time that had passed since the massacre, the two still had issues sleeping. Even their blossoming relationship was not enough to temper their nightmares. They would often just lay there trying to sleep, and failing, until exhaustion eventually set in. They were perpetually tired and despite assurances from their therapists that it was quite common to happen for those suffering from post-traumatic stress, it did not make their fear of sleep any less significant.

Leaving the curtains open helped a little, much like a night-light, and in the current moonlit ambience Gillian studied her boyfriend's face. The scarring was still fresh but, much to Nick's joy, his nose had taken and was healing nicely. There was still pain when he smiled but the doctor said that would disappear in time.

Slowly but surely, they were healing.

"Can't sleep?" Nick asked.

Gillian shook her head.

"He's still there when I shut my eyes," she said.

"Same," Nick said. "Feels like he's always there."

"Yeah." Gillian shuddered. There were times she expected to see him stood in her bedroom watching her sleep, or ready to pull back the curtain when she was in the shower. To be there ready and waiting for when she was at her most vulnerable.

"Can you see me?" said Conrad.

Gillian's stomach lurched and her eyes went wide at the familiar voice that emanated from Nick's mouth. Her man was smiling, though it was not his smile. His eyes were not his eyes.

"Nick?" she asked, terrified.

"Look harder," said Conrad through her boyfriend as the scarring on his nose and cheek began to split. Where bone and muscle and tendons should have been was another face, one that was not Nick's, and it was stubbornly pushing through. The skin of Nick's face loosened as if detached from the skull beneath, and as the *thing* before her continued its vicious, knowing grin, it raised a hand, took hold of the now open scars and pulled. There was wet tearing, as the thing removed the facsimile of Nick, the skin that was not skin separating completely from the head to show Conrad Ellis underneath, bloody and maniacal.

"It should be you on the other end of this knife," Conrad said as his hand reappeared over his head with the carving knife he had used on Gillian pointed toward her face. It was glistening with blood, fresh blood, that Gillian knew was hers.

She opened her mouth to scream and was met with silence.

He brought it down quick.

★

Her mother was there when Gillian woke to the sound of her own terrified screams. She tried desperately to hush her daughter and failed.

It was still her bedroom, though she was alone in her bed. No Nick, and certainly no Conrad, but for the briefest of moments she was sure the throbbing behind her eyes was the result of a knife to her face.

She continued to scream until she lost her voice, and even then, they came in whispers.

Her mother held her for the duration.

ACKNOWLEDGEMENTS

So, here it is. My very first full-length novel. It's quite a different experience from writing short stories or novellas but I'd argue it's more rewarding. It wasn't quite what I expected my first novel to be – I had planned to write a ghost story called *Croft House* or a supernatural novel called *The Eyeless* - but it was great fun to write all the same.

As with all projects, there are many people to thank.

I must give a special shout out to the people in the indie-writing community. There are a good few of you out there who, like me, are just trying to get their work seen and they have been enormously encouraging. The few of you I speak to on a regular basis, thank you for your encouragement and notes. I hope I've been able to reciprocate in kind.

I should probably note that, as a Brit, setting this book in the Pacific northwest did present a few challenges, mainly how police matters are dealt with, legal jurisdictions, that kind of thing, and I'm 100% sure there are errors all over the place regarding this. The errors are all mine, and some are deliberate to ensure the plot moves.

I want to thank my family again for their support. Again, my parents are keen for me to write children's literature, but they're still happy I'm doing something I love.

Thanks to my stepsister Kate, who's knack for proof reading is invaluable. If there are any error in this manuscript, they're from changes I've made after she returned the draft to me.

I'm at a stage now where I have some genuine fans, which is a surreal experience. I wasn't particularly happy with my previous book, *Office Politics*, but there were still kind words said about it none the less and for that I thank you. As this journey continues, I want you all to be honest in your criticisms. I'm keen to get better and notes are always welcome.

And, as always, to Charlotte, my fiancée and life partner. She, again, took to editing this work for me and her notes were both informative and brutal. I love our editing sessions and I know she does too. But, most importantly, your presence in my life just makes every day all the better for having you in them. Thank you for being you.

Printed in Great Britain
by Amazon